Axis Stone Mysteries

THE GIRL WITH THE LUNATIC FRINGE

G. L. Keady

Published in Australia in 2023
by Big Island Publishing

Big Island Publishing
PO Box 3027, Tuross Head, 2537, NSW, Australia.
www.bigislandpublishing.au

ISBN:
E-book: 978-0-6459739-7-6
Print: 978-0-6459738-4-6

Edited by: Canon Doyle
Cover design and art: Brandon Evans-Keady

This book is dedicated to the cherished memory
of my dear friend, S.J.C Powell.

Rest in Peace, Powelly.

TABLE OF CONTENTS

CHAPTER
ONE

Spring in New York is something else, simply gorgeous. I think coming out of a harsh winter makes springtime feel even more pleasurable. The short walk to the office felt invigorating this day. I was mulling over the events of the last case, still adrift with no clear explanation of what had occurred. It's my form to rationalise things, and the whole demon thing, Danny's voices, the vision I'd shared with Angel—all pointed to something that was beyond logic. I resolved to just move on by filing it under 'unexplained', at least it had a resolution.

I hadn't heard from Charlie or Nick since we took our respective flights home from Belize.

I grabbed a copy of the daily Metro and the weekly Villager newspapers from the newsstand, along with my daily supply of gum. The Newsie was getting to know me and my habits. I think my saying "Thanks, mate," an Aussie thing, made me stand out a little more than his run-of-the-mill customer, who notoriously seemed to carry the burden of the world on their shoulders with seriously unfriendly, dour expressions and mannerisms.

I was looking forward to sitting in my office chair, catching up with the local news, sipping a freshly brewed coffee, and munching on a croissant. The anticipation of Kendy spoiling me with those things made my tummy growl.

As I stepped into the lobby of the Regis Building, I changed hands holding the papers to shake hands with Linus, who was on his way out. In doing so, the word 'death' in the front-page headline of the Metro caught my curious eye.

"Good to have you back, son, you've got a tan," Linus said.

Though the radiation effects were wearing off, I'd been left with a welcomed suntan. None of us, with the exception of Doctor Flowers, had the blisters and peeling skin like the first time we'd experienced the beam of light.

"A few days in the Yucatan sun quickly replaced my Manhattan complexion. How are you doing, Linus?"

"Oh, you know, getting old doesn't come with a manual, so there's a new surprise every day. This morning I was eating that healthy cereal, whatever you call it, sounds German..."

"Muesli..."

"Yes, that stuff, horse food Book calls it ... anyhow, I bit down on a nut and smashed a molar. Fantastic, most expensive breakfast I've ever had ... on my way to the dentist now for repairs. They charge like wounded bulls, those dentists."

"Got insurance?" I asked.

"If it didn't come in the cereal box, then no."

I chuckled, enjoying his sense of humour.

"Book's been keeping me abreast of your last case. What about that guy with the two voices in his head?"

"Danny, yeah, pretty strange."

"I thought it was bad enough having one in my head, but two? ... Oh, did you hear about the local death? It was on the radio this morning."

"Old habits die hard, eh? Still listening to the radio," I said while unfurling the newspaper. "Yes, it's made the headlines in the Metro. A member of a local rock band, The Lunatic Fringe, found dead after a gig, cops claim overdose."

"Yeah, the kids in that band used to play around in the lobby here when they were whippersnappers... they'd make me come out and chase 'em off. I used to enjoy that. Terrible loss now she's grown up, to die like that. Anyhow, better get to my appointment, don't wanna keep the White Angel waiting."

I watched him hobble off, thinking about his reference to the White Angel as his dentist. Then, it hit me; the Nazi torturer in the '70s movie "Marathon Man", starring Dustin Hoffman. I chuckled, doing my cardiac exercise ascending the staircase.

The rich aroma of brewing coffee punched me in the nose the very second I set foot on the landing to my floor.

I opened the door, expecting to find the smiling face of Kendy, but instead found her crying. I went to her and gave her a hug. "What's up, mate?"

She looked up at me with eyes that seemed to have been crying for hours and squeezed out between sobs, "Dwip's dead."

Dwip was her girlfriend. I walked her to the couch. "Argh, hell, sit down, love. Tell me what happened."

"Dwip played keys for the Lunatic Fringe ... they just had a minor hit song ... I was at their gig at the Bitter End last night..."

"The Bitter End?"

"In the Village, been around since the 60s, only fits a couple of hundred." She blew her nose, calming down somewhat as she talked it through.

"Right, go on," I said, filling two mugs with coffee and grabbing two croissants. Kendy waved her hand no to a croissant. I handed her a mug and sat down opposite.

"Dwip formed the band with Rag Doll, the lead singer ... the five of them grew up together here. I was a member of the gang. We all did school together and hung out. I used to go to their rehearsals and stuff, even worked on a few of their songs with Dwip," she said with a teary smile.

"So it was an all-girl band?"

"Yep, a queer band, you know, with songs about queer stuff and all. It attracted queer followers. So, like, I went to the gig with Dwip. She liked me to help set up her keyboards and computer, like a roadie ... But she was a bit weird on the way there in the van, like distant. So I asked her..."

~ ~ ~

I was driving the white Ford Transit van, with Dwip seated beside me in the passenger seat. I'd been laughing at her jet-black spiked hair, vividly tipped in a spectrum of rainbow colours. Already adorned in her stage gear of leathers, studded belts, and chains, she presented a BDSM aesthetic, which clashed intriguingly with her rainbow-hued hair. Absorbed in thought, she gazed at the traffic ahead, rhythmically chewing gum.

"What's wrong, babe? You're like off with the pixies," I said.

She was on the verge of responding when her ringtone, the Fringe's song 'Femme Fatale', interrupted her. A text had arrived. She read it, and a look of concern suddenly etched itself across her face.

"What's wrong, babe? You're like off with the pixies," I observed, a note of worry in my voice.

"Someone's been cyberstalking me ... I didn't mention it, thinking they'd just lose interest, but since 'Femme Fatale' began gaining airplay, the harassment's escalated."

"Is it a guy? A chick?" I enquired.

"I dunno... doesn't specify."

"What did the message say just now?"

"Just random shit."

"Dwip, come on... I can tell when you're bottling things up."

"It said I'm gonna die tonight, alright?" She snapped, her voice taut with tension.

"What the fuck! That's serious man ... why didn't you mention this earlier! We need to contact Bulldog at the NYPD or someone, immediately..."

"Take it easy, Ken, it's alright ... it's probably just a fan overstepping the mark ... perhaps someone approached me after a gig, I didn't notice, and they took offence. It comes with the territory."

"Have you spoken to Rag Doll about this?" I asked, concern lacing my voice.

"I vaguely mentioned it; she said to tell the new manager, what's-his-name."

"Devon Steel?"

"Yeah, that's him. I've not met him yet."

I steered the van into the loading bay of the Bitter End.

"He'll be here tonight, won't he?" I queried, my tone laced with concern.

"Supposed to be. I'll speak to him after our set."

"Promise?"

"Absolutely."

We shared a quick kiss before disembarking to load in.

~ ~ ~

I'd finished my croissant. Kendy raised an eyebrow at me. "You can have mine."

That was an invite I couldn't refuse. I got up to fetch it. "Keep talking…"

"Well, there was nothing odd about the gig. Usual crowd, maybe a few more since the band was getting better known. I was standing next to the mixing console when a dude came up beside me and shouted, "Vocals are too loud!"'"

"Don't tell me, I'm not doing sound!" I shouted back. "Who are you anyway?"

I'd already worked out he must be Devon Steel, the new manager. He looked and was acting pretty obnoxious.

"I'm the manager, Devon Steel," he said pompously with a British accent. He went up to Zippo, the sound guy, and yelled in his ear. Zippo didn't look impressed, and the two of them had words. I couldn't hear it; the vocals were too loud. But you know, Fringe is a loud punk band, like what do you expect?"

"How old is he?" I asked.

"Mid-twenties, short-cropped dyed white hair, facial fluff, good looking ... he was wearing a shiny grey suit and a pencil-thin necktie ... totally Carnaby Street," Kendy said. "He wandered off to the bar ... The band got to their single 'Femme Fatale', and the crowd went off. When they finished, they got an encore to play it again. Dwip waved me up on stage, so I jumped up and sang backing vocals. It was a good gig.

When we went backstage, there was music press hanging at the door, being handled by Devon. We pushed through and left Rag Doll with them.

The usual suspects were in the dressing room. It's just one room a table, a few chairs, mirrors and stuff, you know the drill."

"Did you know them all?" I questioned.

"Yeah, I guess so. There was one I didn't know, she was a bit pushy, a friend of the lead guitar, Slick."

"Nice names they have."

"Yeah, they were our nicknames from school. Rag Doll was always the ringleader. Her real name's Kelly. You've seen her; she works at Rudy's Music Store up on Broome Street."

"Yeah, she sold me some guitar strings. Mad hair, Goth dresser, right?"

"That's Rag."

"Want another coffee?" I asked.

"No thanks, I'm wired to the max."

"I'm not," I said, getting up for a refill. "Carry on."

"Zippo dropped us at Dwip's apartment in the van. Dwip was dog-tired, so we said goodnight, and I walked home. Next thing, I get a call from Bla at like 8 AM, saying she'd been to Dwip's to drop off her phone she'd left at the gig and found her on the bathroom floor, dead."

"That must have been like 7 AM for the newspapers to get it into the headlines."

Kendy blew her nose on a tissue tearing up again. "Yeah, that'd be right. Bla had an 8 AM start. She 'd sometimes swing past on her way to work ... Dwip, she was an early riser."

"So it was an overdose? Was she a user?"

"No! That's what's so wrong. Dwip never went near drugs, especially since her older brother like OD'd two years ago. Can we take the case? Please."

"Case? we can't, not until the cops are done. Besides, I can't say I'm hip to the queer community," I admitted.

"Hey, it's me you're talking to. You can like cut any situation," she appealed.

I felt I couldn't say no to Kendy; she's family, and Dwip was her partner. "Let me talk to Bulldog, okay? Go home and chill. Come in tomorrow, I should know something by then."

She'd no sooner walked out the door when my The Terrible Tango ringtone played—it was Bulldog.

"G'Day Bulldog, I was wondering how long it'd take before you rang."

"How's Kendy taking it?" he said in a three pack a day voice.

"I sent her home, she's pretty cut up. How do you read it?"

"Vice figured it as an OD, but it didn't add up for me."

"Why?"

"No jab marks, no kit, not a known user, not a drug in the apartment except for her meds … Tox isn't back yet, but I'll put my house on her being clean."

"So, what are you thinking?"

"I'm thinking murder."

"How?"

"That's the conundrum, nothing obvious."

"Kendy wants me to investigate, will I get in your way?"

"Never, my friend. You can stick your nose where I can't. As long as you keep me up to speed, go for it."

I had his blessing. Always up for a challenge, I phoned Booker to get a heads up on toxicology.

CHAPTER TWO

I couldn't believe it could take a month to get a toxicology report. According to Book, the autopsy would be completed in a day, and he had a friend of a friend who would get me the inside scoop on the result. I left it to Book to handle and focused on talking to Bla, the bass player in the band, who had found the body. I phoned Kendy and got Bla's number; she told me her real name is Zola. Bla is an acronym for a black lesbian.

I phoned Zola, and she agreed to meet me at her day job: the Vanilla Gorilla Café in Hell's Kitchen.

The walk there would do me good.

My mental picture of Zola, the bass player in a female punk band, was shattered when I asked the pretty African-American girl behind the café counter if Zola was around. Of course, she was Zola. Der. She, however, took it in good spirits and joined me at a table. I checked the specials and asked what she recommended. She knew from Kendy I was a croissant nut, but I'd already overindulged with two, so she suggested trying a homemade brownie. Being a dark chocolate devotee, I took her up on it.

"Must've been a shock finding Dwip this morning. Are you okay?"

"A bit numb really, like I wanted to go home and chill but couldn't change shifts."

"Do you mind running me through everything from leaving the gig last night to finding her?"

"Sure."

Her workmate brought the brownie. I tasted it and acknowledged, "Hmm, nice." My intention was to mentally visualise her story, a skill I'd developed of late that seemed to work.

Zola started, "After Dwip left with Kendy and Zippo in the van, I walked home. I've got a studio apartment in the village, nothing flash, mind you. So I got in at 1:30 AM. I remember the time 'coz I had to set my alarm for 6 AM. Normally, I don't have an early start after a late gig, but like I said, I wasn't able to change my shift—"

Dressed in her work gear, Zola left her apartment block. "I left home and walked to Dwip's place; it ain't far, along the way to work. I knew she'd been needing her phone ... she'd left it backstage—not like her to leave her phone anywhere.

"It was the usual packed pavement for that time of day. Nothing out of the ordinary. I got to Dwip's apartment and was just about to press the buzzer when a delivery guy came out, so I slipped into the lobby and caught the elevator to her floor. No-one in the corridor, got to her door, knocked, and the door swung open; unlocked ... again, not like Dwip, she was seriously paranoid about burglars, I guess with all her computers, instruments, and stuff ... I went in, called out for her ... nothing. 'Dwip?' I called again, and went to the bedroom. The bed was made ... which I thought was odd, then I looked towards the en-suite ... the door was open a bit, and I could see her hand like on the floor. I pushed the door open ... and—"

The memory of it had upset her; she started to cry. "It's okay,' I said sympathetically. "I'm sorry to put you through this."

She gathered herself together and said, "It's pretty much what I told the cops. I'm the one that called them ... Dwip was still dressed in her stage gear except her knickers were around her knees like she'd been having a pee when ... Um, oh, one thing I've just remembered and didn't tell the cops, her keyboard was in its road-case in the middle of the living room."

"Why was that unusual?"

"Oh man, she'd never leave it there, she had OCD big time,

meticulous about putting everything in its like right place. Made me think someone had been with her and maybe distracted her or something."

"Anything else odd?"

"Yeah, she only had one boot on, her other foot was bare."

"Was the other boot there?"

"Yeah, on the bedroom floor with the sock, but she always went barefoot around the apartment, insisted on leaving your shoes just inside the door. You know, I think it was the Japanese in her."

"Oh, I'd assumed she was originally from China?"

"Nar, nar, second-generation AJ ... her grandparents had been imprisoned here during the Second World War."

"So what did the cops have to say?"

"Oh man, that was like painful, they took like forever to get there ... didn't much enjoy being in the apartment with a dead body... you know, it was kinda creepy."

"At least it wasn't gory," I said.

"Yeah, but still."

"So, what did the cops have to say?"

"When they did arrive the place was crawling with them ... not like you see on TV, you know the cops are supposed to not touch anything or leave prints ... these cops didn't give a crap. At first, they treated me like I was the perp, then a detective turned up ... his name was..." she pulled a calling card from her pocket and checked it. "Um, Reece Robinson."

"And what did he have to say?"

"After like one look at Dwip he said it was an OD."

"Right."

She made the cops sound unprofessional, but that might have been due to her emotional state. When it's someone you know found dead, you expect more from everyone ... to the cops, it's just another Jane Doe. It's how they have to react; otherwise, their job would send them round the bend. It was detective Robinson's gig to document the crime scene, not really to formally determine the cause of death, but probably to take an educated punt at it.

"That's about all really … they let me go after like half an hour, I got here a bit late but that was cool."

"You've been very helpful, Zola. Can I ask you one more thing?"

"Sure, go ahead."

"Did Dwip ever mention to you she was being cyberstalked?"

"No … but you know, I figured something was wrong … she'd been getting heaps of calls. Like the other night at rehearsals, her phone never stopped ringing … and like she kept ignoring it and getting pissed. I figure that's why she left her phone … Oh, I forgot, just a sec…"

She jumped up, went to the counter, and returned with a phone. "Here, I forgot to give this to the cops. It's Dwip's phone."

The phone was evidence, so I really couldn't hang onto it. However, my curiosity was getting the better of me, so I rushed back to the office to go through the phone logs.

There were plenty of surprises in the text section; she was definitely being cyberstalked. There were two hundred texts, starting from a month ago. No reply number, and all of them were just a few words, all abusive and increasingly threatening. The last text, at 6 PM, said, 'I'm going to kill you'. That must've been the text Dwip told Kendy about in the van. It was difficult to determine if they were from a male or a female, but if I were to hazard a guess just by the nature of the language, I'd say female. You'd expect a male to choose different obscenities. I checked the logs … mostly calls to numbers in her address book. But on the night of the gig, there were six incoming calls that registered as 'no number'… they were spaced about an hour apart, starting at 6:15 PM. Only the last call at 12:35 AM had been answered, and only for 5 seconds. There were no outgoing calls at all since 6:15 PM. Reading into that scenario, it seemed the killer had issued a threat with the 6:15 PM text, then proceeded to call every hour. By the time of the last call, the killer would have known that the gig had finished. Therefore, if the plan was to ambush Dwip, determining when she'd be getting home wouldn't have been difficult. Agreeing with Kendy and Zola's conclusion, I was convinced that Dwip had been murdered.

~ ~ ~

While on the phone, Bulldog saw me approaching and waved me into his office. I took the chair opposite him behind his desk and waited for him to finish up.

"Hey, big fella, how you doing?"

"Dying for a smoke," he said, struggling out of his chair. "Walk this way."

I got up. "I can't, mate. You've got a particular gait."

He chuckled over his shoulder at me as he led me through the open-plan part of the NYPD, through the fire door onto the smoking balcony. I closed the door behind us and looked down. The ground was littered with cigarette butts. "These all yours?"

"Probably," he mumbled past the cigarette between his lips, lighting up. "Man, if I don't smoke, I eat; if I eat, I die."

"Chewing gum maybe?"

"Can't stand the stuff, makes a person resemble a tumble dryer."

I found that pretty funny. The sincerity of his admission wasn't lost on me, knowing he was diabetic. I handed him a phone.

"The gal who rang you guys forgot to hand this in. It's Dwip's phone. Mate, I chatted with Kendy, then Bla or Zola, her real name—she'd only been at Dwip's to drop off her phone because she'd left it at the gig last night. Bla is the bass player of The Lunatic Fringe, Dwip played keys."

"I'll give this to IT to check out, thanks."

"I can tell you now, she was murdered for sure. There are incriminating texts on the phone. Kendy and Zola confirmed Dwip wasn't into drugs … I know it's tempting to expect she was, being in a punk rock band and all, but her brother died from an overdose two years ago, and the memory of that has kept her clean."

"So you suspect a cyberstalker?"

"Sure do … fits the MO and the threats."

"No wounds, no bullet holes?"

"Knickers around the knees, still in her stage gear, on the floor, one shoe off, the other one on, her keyboard in the road-case left in the middle of the living room…"

Bulldog was nodding slowly as he took a big draw on his ciggy. "So, what does that tell you?" he said, exhaling a stream of smoke.

"I'd say she came home from the gig with Kendy, was busting for a pee, rushed into her apartment, didn't lock the door, left her road-case in the living room, made it just in time to the bathroom, sat on the John, took off her shoe and sock, was about to take off the other one when, whack-o! she gets ambushed."

Bulldog extinguished the cigarette butt between his fingers. "Makes sense, but we'll only know after the autopsy. Any luck the stalker left a number?"

"Nope, but I think by the language of the texts, the stalker's a woman."

He led me back inside and stopped me at the elevator. "Talk to Kendy … see if she knows any more about the stalker … maybe she's got an idea who it is, especially with you thinking it's a she. You know these queer types, they can have all sorts of funky scenes going on, you get what I'm saying?"

"Funky scenes … now that's showing your age. Cool bananas. Ciao, my friend."

As I stepped into the elevator, he said, "I'll take Robinson off the case, he's not right for it. I'll take it from here," he concluded with a wink, which meant he was leaving it to me.

CHAPTER
THREE

Zola finished work and was walking home when 'Femme Fatale' started playing from the back pocket of her jeans. She pulled out her phone, kept walking, and answered, "Hello, you've got Zola. Speak up now or forever hold your tongue."

"You can be funny, can't you? I want to meet you."

"Name, please?"

"When we meet. I've desired you from afar."

"How did you get my number?"

"A friend."

Zola stopped in her tracks.

"Send a photo, otherwise there's no chance."

"Click this link."

Her phone beeped with an incoming message. The call had terminated. She checked the text; it was a URL to download an app. Curiosity got the better of her, and she selected it. After a moment, a scarlet Yoni flower materialised on the screen. She knew what it looked like but wondered what it represented. Intrigued, she clicked on it, and the app opened. Another beep sounded, a text. She checked it. The text read, 'Meet me. I've got eyes on you.' Now, she was in a real panic.

~ ~ ~

Kendy was curled up on the sofa, watching TV. Her eyes were swollen from crying. She hadn't moved for hours, glued to staring but not watching, reminiscing about the two wonderful years she'd spent with Dwip. Her phone broke the reverie. Her hand crept out from under the blanket draped over her and collected the phone from the coffee table.

"Hey, Bla."

"Hey Ken, you okay?"

"Hangin' in, you?"

"Like, still stunned … just going home."

"You talked with Axis … all good?"

"Yep, he's cool … makes you feel safe, don't he?"

"Yep, he sure does."

"I gave him Dwip's phone, forgot to give it to the cops."

"He'll probably give it to them."

"Hey listen, have you had any, like, weirdo calls today?"

Kendy sat up and yawned. "No, why?"

"This chick called me, said she got my number from a friend, wanted to meet. I said no. She sent me a link, I opened it and it downloaded an app. The she sent me another text demanding to meet, said she's got eyes on me, like creepy."

"She might be Dwip's killer! Trash the app."

"I can't, I can't, it won't delete. Every time I try, when I reopen, it's back again."

"Are you home yet?"

"No, nearly."

"Then come here, I'll ring Axis," Kendy said hurriedly. "Don't stop, don't talk to anyone, don't answer your phone, okay Bla?"

"Okay. I'll be there like in 10 minutes."

Kendy hung up and immediately rang me. I was at the office when The Terrible Tango sounded. I answered and immediately hightailed it out of there for Kendy's place. On the way, I called Bulldog and gave him an update.

Kendy let me in, and Zola was on the lounge looking quite

distressed. She explained what had happened and then showed me the app.

"Hey, look at this," Kendy said. "I've somehow got that app as well." She flashed us her screen, sure enough, there was the red Yoni Flower.

"I don't get it; how could you have it?" Zola questioned.

"I didn't download it," Kendy said, mystified. "Wait a minute, check your phone, Axis."

I looked and, sure enough, I had the app as well. "I get it, the original phone that downloads the app then passes it via a bot to whoever is called..." I guessed.

"And then the bot installs the app. How smart is that?" Kendy said.

"Frightening. I called Rag Doll, Slick, and Butch to talk about our next gig, now their phones would be affected," Zola said.

"And so it goes," I exclaimed. "Shit, I called Bulldog. How many phone calls would he have made since?"

Kendy was madly fingering her screen. "No matter what, I can't trash it ... it just keeps coming back."

"Turn off the WiFi and trash it," I said, trying the same myself. It worked, but as soon as connectivity was resumed, it reappeared. "This is ridiculous. I need to get it to an IT boffin quick smart."

"Did you explore the app, Bla?" Kendy asked.

"Negative, it freaked me out."

"No, don't open it, not until I've had it looked at," I cautioned. "Zola, text the band members and anyone else you called not to open the app or call anyone."

"Do you think it's like listening to us? Like, I mean, it's obviously tracking us ... but what else can it do?"

"It's seriously sophisticated, Kendy, so nothing would surprise me. By now the compounding effect of phones infecting other phones would be in the hundreds, if not thousands ... this thing is a virus." I took out my satellite phone, which I carried for contacting my partners Charlie and Nick. To avoid further infection, I rang the

NYPD and had them put me through to Bulldog on his landline. I filled him in. He checked his cellphone, and sure enough, he had the app. He would get it immediately to the IT department he'd given Dwip's phone to.

Kendy had her laptop out and searched the URL of the app. There was nothing on it.

"It's obviously pure malware," she said.

"Explain," I requested.

"Software that is specifically designed to disrupt, damage, or gain unauthorized access to a computer system, in this case, a phone. So, yes, it is in fact a virus like you said, and it'd be like exponential."

"Hell, so within hours it could infect like millions of phones," Zola said.

I flopped into an armchair to think out loud, "So, you'd have to think Dwip's phone wasn't infected, otherwise it would have passed the virus on to you guys."

"So it started with me?" Zola declared, shocked.

"It's okay, love, no fault of yours," Kendy said, trying to calm her.

"But if I hadn't downloaded it..."

"It was obviously going to happen anyway, Zola," I said. "Thing of it is, what's the intention? On one hand, whoever this is has some sort of vendetta against the band ... and on the other hand, she launched something that can affect zillions of phones."

"Yeah, like, what's the point of it?" Kendy seconded.

"Okay, okay," I said as I stood up. "First things first ... I think the virus is merely a distraction; the real target appears to be the band members. So, that's where our focus should lie."

"I just received a text from Rag Doll; her phone's infected," Zola added.

I paced the floor, then stopped. "Okay, listen up. Who murdered Dwip? If this individual is targeting band members, why? Do you know her? Are we certain it's a woman?"

"Heck, it could be anyone ... there's no shortage of band detractors and homophobes out there," Zola grumbled.

"You mean lesbophobes," Kendy corrected.

"Perhaps she wanted to join the band and was rejected, or maybe she was a former member you kicked out?" I speculated.

"There have been plenty who wanted to join, but they were musicians. I really don't think they'd murder us over it ... as for the previous band member, no, Kendy was the only one who didn't make it, and that was only because she had a kid to look after," Zola explained.

"True," Kendy affirmed.

"Okay, what about the unrequited love angle? An ex-lover, perhaps?" I suggested.

"No, that theory doesn't hold ... she would have had to have harboured affection for all of us in the band," Zola dismissed.

"But she only contacted you and Dwip," Kendy stated.

"Yeah, so far," Zola replied, expectantly.

"Right, we need to enhance security for the band while we uncover this perp's identity. I'll liaise with the cops. Is there a secure place where the band could stay together, Kendy included?"

"Hey, what about that old house in Jersey Rag mentioned for rehearsal a while back? Remember, Ken?"

"Oh yeah, the house Rag inherited from her grandmother."

"That'll do, provided the perp can't track you there," I advised. "How about you collect the phones from Rag, Slick, and...?"

"Butch, the drummer," Zola supplied.

"Get them to me, and then head to the house for a few days?"

"Sounds practical. We could bring acoustic instruments and work on some songs," Kendy proposed.

"We'll need to inform our new manager, Devon."

"Text him to swing by my office at say 7. Get yourselves there as well ... that'll give me time to go see Bulldog ... can you coordinate that, Kendy?"

"Yep, Butch has a car, doesn't she, Zola?"

"If you can call it that. But yeah, it'll get us there."

I moved towards the door. "Stay alert, and remember, no phone calls, no sketchy people, okay?" At the door, Zola halted me.

"What if someone like Ken's mother calls?" Zola inquired.

"Answer only if you recognise the caller ID. No outgoing calls. Once you're at the office, you can use the landline to let folks know, but the fewer who know the actual location of where you'll be, the better. Understood?"

They nodded, and I departed.

~ ~ ~

The NYPD was in chaos when I arrived on Bulldog's homicide level. Bulldog was in his office on the phone, red-faced as if he was about to explode. Aware I was probably responsible for the disorder, I made sure he could see me through the window ... he waved me in.

"I don't give a rat's ass!" he shouted into the phone. "Hire him! ... her...!" He slammed down the phone.

"You okay, mate? Don't have a coronary on my account," I declared.

"Sit down, no, better still ... follow me," he headed out of the office, and I followed closely behind. "I'm not going to say 'walk this way'..." he joked.

"What's the situation?"

"Chaos. Everyone with a mobile phone has what they're calling 'the pussy app.' They've all been barred from using their phones, sent them into meltdown."

"Where are we headed?"

"To the tech team. They've hired a tech whiz to tackle this app."

We navigated through the building to a secluded area where tech experts congregated.

In a dimly lit room, a young Asian woman was surrounded by tech personnel.

One of the boffins introduced her, "Bulldog, this is Lucy Yip."

Without looking up at us, Lucy kept on keying at a blistering speed, "Do I call you Bulldog or just plain, Dog?" she asked.

"No preference ... This is Axis Stone, everyone ... he'll know more about this stuff than me."

"They call me the Yipster," she said, not looking up from her keyboard.

"So, what do we know, Yipster?" I asked.

"The code is exceptionally sophisticated," she replied with a slight accent.

"Its capabilities?" I inquired.

"Whatever a phone can do, it can do … exploiting every function."

"Is it local?"

"Yes, originating from New York, but its exact location is untraceable."

"So, we can't disable it?" Bulldog asked.

"Only the creator can. It's AI, learning and adapting. It's unstoppable. Pretty soon government, CIA, Homeland Security, the FBI, you name it, they'll be all over it. This thing could launch missiles if it wanted to ... start a freaking war."

"Spreading all over the world," I stated grimly.

Lucy stopped typing and looked up seriously, "Axis, the pussy app is a worldwide threat with no apparent solution."

CHAPTER
FOUR

When I entered my office, it was bustling with activity. Kendy was conversing animatedly with the remaining four members of Lunatic Fringe and their manager, Devon. The chatter subsided as Kendy made the introductions.

"Everyone, this is my boss, Axis."

I greeted each of them individually. "Rag, and you must be Slick and..."

Zola chimed in, "Butch. The drummer."

I concluded with the manager, "Devon." His handshake was limp, diminishing my initial impression of him.

"Let me brief you on what I've learned. The police have enlisted an IT expert to investigate the app, now dubbed 'the pussy app.'" The band members exchanged amused glances.

Kendy refocused the group. "Quieten down, let's hear him out."

"It's unstoppable and can manipulate any phone function. As for Dwip's attacker, we're clueless. The cause of death remains unknown until after the autopsy tomorrow."

"Rag believes she may know who's responsible," Kendy interjected.

Rag, with her striking features and commanding presence, certainly stood out. Her gothic style accentuated her dramatic appearance. I could see why she was the lead—she had a photogenic allure.

"I accessed the app. There's a 'play' option leading to an AI-generated music video of our song, 'Femme Fatale.' It's not us performing, yet it eerily mimics our style. A prompt to purchase the song for fifty cents in cryptocurrency appears after a short preview. So far it's been downloaded six hundred thousand times."

Devon was quick to calculate, "That's three hundred thousand dollars! This is outright theft."

The situation was taking on a new dimension with the worldwide attention Dwip's death and the app were garnering. It was a scam of monumental proportions.

"It's making us famous," Slick remarked.

Rag agreed, "Publicity like this is priceless."

"Global," Zola added.

"Yeah, but at what expense? Dwip's gone, and we're being exploited," Butch countered, her rough demeanour hinting at an upbringing tougher than the others.

Their discussions overlapped chaotically until I intervened. "Time out!" I demanded. "So, Rag, this app led you to a suspect?"

"Yep, Zippo."

"Ah, come on Rag, we went to school with Zippo, besides he helped us bump out last night, while you were doing all the press, with Steel-baby here," Butch growled. It wasn't hard to tell who wore the pants in the band.

Rag conceded, "True."

Butch continued, "You're just sore because he caught you with your groupie."

"Suzie?" Rag acknowledged sheepishly.

"So, no clear suspects then?" I prodded.

Slick, her face obscured by her wild hair, spoke up. "I got a threatening text like Bla's."

"Show me, Slick," I requested.

I read aloud from her phone, "Meet me tonight or you'll end up like Dwip."

"Did you respond?" I asked.

"No way," Slick snapped.

"Can't we reply and trace the number?" Devon suggested, sounding exasperated.

"A text contains location data, but tracing it requires a specific app," I explained.

"I have a tracker," Rag offered.

"If she designed the pussy app, she's likely using encryption to conceal her identity," Kendy pointed out.

"I could reply and attend the meeting alone," I suggested.

"Isn't that a bit risky, considering what happened to Dwip?" Devon asked, concerned.

"It's part of my job," I affirmed.

"He's always doing stuff like that," Kendy remarked nonchalantly.

"Okay, we'll try it," I decided.

While Kendy was getting them ready to leave, I rang Bulldog on the landline and explained my plan.

"I don't like it, Axis. At least wait until we get a result from the autopsy … we still can't confirm it was murder, and if it was, we don't know what the murderer is capable of."

"I hear you. I'll hold off until then," I confirmed.

I filled him in about the band being ripped off by the pussy app, which he agreed could be a motive. After hanging up, I updated everyone on the change in plan and got no objections.

"Is your mum looking after the little one?" I asked Kendy.

"Yeah."

"Use the satellite phone Carmen got you."

"Speaking of Carmen, might be worth bringing her in on this. She's like good with IT."

"Good thinking. I'll ring them once you lot are out of here. Did Nick sign the agreement?"

"Yes, sent all the signed copies to Charlie yesterday. So it's official, we're now Stone, Vargas, and Chan. Nick said his daughter Michelle will be handling the Manila office."

"Did he give you the address?"

"Yeah, you'll love it."

"Why?"

"He bought a boat moored at the Manila Yacht Club."

"What, the office is on a boat? Is he trying to make sure I'll never visit?"

She laughed.

They left their phones with me, but I had to threaten Devon to get his. Typical manager, always needing to be in touch.

Once they left, the place felt peaceful. Thinking about dinner, I first decided to give Charlie a call on the satellite phone.

"Hey, Kendy said it's all official."

"Yes, partner, it is. We're cracking a bottle of bubbly right now ... actually, we just landed our first case."

"Excellent, tell me about it?"

"A famous actor is being blackmailed."

"Do I know him?"

"Her. Serina Sun."

"Wow, yeah, she's a looker. What's she being blackmailed over?"

"Some compromising CCTV footage she'd rather keep from her employer and fans. Guess what else?"

"What?"

"We've got Enzo Ciprani working for us. The guy's got a real nose for this kind of work."

I told him about my case. He was surprised, as it was already big news in LA. I said I could use Carmen's IT skills. He agreed to put her on a flight to meet me at Bulldog's NYPD office in the morning. We laughed about Nick's new office and agreed he did it to spite me. Thinking of Enzo reminded me of Patricia, so I decided to give her a call.

~ ~ ~

It didn't take long for telecom companies worldwide to filter out the pussy app at their servers. Despite its widespread initial invasion of millions of cellphones, the story lingered in the disposable news services for only a day. Nevertheless, this brief exposure was enough to catapult The Lunatic Fringe into fame and earn the app's creator a fortune from downloads of the song 'Femme Fatale.' For Devon Steel, the challenge lay in associating the song with the band; the music charts credited 'Pussy App' as the artist, and the public followed suit. This situation was frustrating for Devon, especially since he was in hiding in Jersey without a phone to sway public opinion or capitalise on the media frenzy. The band's absence, with no spokesperson to clarify their position, swiftly turned them into an enigma. From their hideout, the band faced the uncertainty of whether Dwip had officially registered the song—another critical question for Axis to resolve.

~ ~ ~

"I'm not convinced this bird's on the level," Enzo growled. It was evening on the West Coast. Enzo, Charlie, and Carmen were gathered in the lounge area of the new Stone, Vargas, and Chan Investigations office on the third floor of 9026 Sunset Boulevard. The West Hollywood office, occupying the entire third floor above LA Guitar Sales and Shamrock Tattoo, had been impressively decorated by Carmen, blending modernity with comfort.

"What gives you that impression, Enzo?" Charlie asked, handing Enzo a beer. He and Carmen were sipping red wine.

"The hotel security claims the CCTV footage of the swimming pool wasn't taken and was auto-erased after seventy-two hours."

"That means someone might've taken it, copied it, and put it back within that time frame," Carmen proposed.

Enzo acknowledged, "Possible."

"What do you think Miss Sun is concealing, Enzo?" Charlie asked.

"It's not just about what she's doing; it's what she's not disclosing ... like the identity of the woman she was with."

"Knowing that won't help us catch the blackmailer," Charlie pointed out.

"Maybe not, but what if she's also being blackmailed?" Enzo

proposed.

Carmen suggested, "It was only a one-night stand. Why is Miss Sun so worried about disclosing her?"

"She's totally paranoid about being dropped from a major movie role if the studio finds out," Enzo explained.

"We're aware she's been confirmed for the part," Charlie said. "What leads do we have on the blackmailer?"

Just then, the receptionist, Carol, with her striking pink hair and white mini skirt, popped in. "Anything else before I leave, Mr Chan?"

"No, Carol, thank you. See you in the morning," Charlie replied.

"Did you hear back from the NYPD?" Carmen inquired.

"Yes, your flight lands at JFK at 9:15 AM. You're expected at homicide by 10:30, traffic permitting."

Carmen smiled appreciatively. "Thanks, Carol."

As Carol left, Enzo couldn't help but admire her shapely legs. She seemed to relish the attention.

"Did you manage to speak with the security guard who was on duty that night?" Charlie inquired of Enzo.

"No, hotel management informed me that Jason Collins contracted COVID a month ago and hasn't returned since. I visited his apartment in Santa Monica today. His neighbour mentioned that Collins hasn't been seen there for a while. He did give me Collins' cell number, though. I used a dirtbox to track it and found he was in New York, but his phone went offline today, probably due to the pussy app chaos there."

"I'll follow up on that while I'm in New York," Carmen offered.

Enzo tapped his phone, and Carmen's phone beeped. "Jason's number," Enzo stated.

Charlie nodded thoughtfully. "It seems we can reasonably suspect Collins as our main person of interest."

"Yeah, look," Enzo summarised, "Miss Sun was with this unknown woman at 3 AM, on a deckchair by the rooftop pool. Collins was on duty, watching on the monitor. He recognises Miss Sun, and possibly the other woman. He either took the tape to be duplicated or recorded the monitor with his phone. Judging by the video quality sent to Miss Sun, it's more likely the latter."

"That's my assessment too," Carmen concurred.

Charlie, agreeing with a nod, finished his glass of wine and stood, signalling the meeting's conclusion. "Thank you, Enzo. Your work is invaluable."

"Give my best to Axis, Carmen. Oh, and the blackmailer is demanding a hundred grand for the video. Does Miss Sun have that kind of money?"

"I'll find out," Charlie assured.

"We all know the best way to catch a blackmailer is to set him up to collect the ransom. This guy ain't no pro. If it's Collins, he's only 24. You get what I'm saying?"

"Loud and clear, Enzo," Charlie said, patting him on the back.

~ ~ ~

I walked out of my apartment block into Wednesday. I've experienced plenty of Wednesdays before, but this one felt unusually distinct. The bustling pedestrians seemed uplifted, their cellphone service restored, reuniting them with their familiar digital lifelines. A day without their devices had likely left many adrift in a state of unease, so entwined were they with their digital portals.

Joining their ranks, I phoned Kendy. "Kendy, is everything alright there? Yep, I'll meet her at eleven. I'll arrange for a courier to deliver all their phones. Just steer clear of the pussy app ... Yes, the autopsy results should be in by this afternoon; Booker is getting me the result. Otherwise, it'll be another day before I hear anything. Hold on, what's Dwip's real name? Can you send me all her details? I'm almost at the office, just stopping to grab a croissant or two ... Talk later."

Settling into my office chair with a croissant and coffee, I received Kendy's text. Dwip's real name was Sonoko Tanaka, 31, single, holding a Master's in Information Technology from New York University, with two siblings; Ren Tanaka, aged 28 and a deceased older brother Hero Tanaka 35. Her parents were also deceased. The origins of her nickname, Dwip, eluded me. A quick search suggested it could mean a state of wilful stupidity or a combination of the dance moves 'whip' and 'dab.' Neither seemed particularly enlightening. Further digging revealed that Sonoko's parents had died in a car accident in 2013 and her brother Ren lived in LA.

~ ~ ~

Later, I entered Bulldog's office. "A bit less chaotic today, mate," I greeted him.

"You're not kidding. It left some carnage in its wake," he replied, swivelling his chair to face me.

"As pussies often do," I quipped.

"Ha! Ain't that the truth. Can you believe that Yipster, charging five hundred bucks an hour, didn't mention that simply having the telecoms filter it out would shut it down?"

"Yeah, she was supposed to be the expert, wasn't she?"

"These tech geniuses ... I read about the animators at Warner Brothers in Burbank once. One executive claimed the smoke from dope drifting from their building got him stoned."

"That explains some of those wild cartoons," I mused.

"I reckon these IT experts are cut from the same cloth."

"Probably, just minus the weed," I added.

Spotting Carmen approaching, I noted, "Here comes a breath of fresh air."

As Bulldog rose from his chair, I introduced her. "Bulldog, meet my colleague from the LA office, Miss Carmen Hu."

With the pleasantries exchanged, we headed to the tech department. Carmen remarked, "This situation really shows how vulnerable our digital world is."

"Indeed, a different kind of hack," I agreed.

Bulldog recalled, "What did Yipster call it? Sophisticated?"

"A gentle way to describe something so destructive. It's like calling COVID clever," Carmen commented disdainfully.

We made our way to the tech department. Bulldog introduced Carmen to Joel, the team leader, then inquired, "Where's Miss Yip?"

"She wrapped up last night. Once the issue was resolved, there wasn't a need to keep her on," Joel responded.

I asked, "Why didn't she suggest the fix that was ultimately used?"

"Mr Stone, what the media reported might've sounded simple, but the solution was incredibly complex. It required intricate coding and a coordinated software update on servers globally—a monumental task," Joel explained.

"I understand that. But why didn't Lucy Yip, with her touted expertise, propose this in theory?" Bulldog persisted.

"I'm not sure about that," Joel admitted, slightly flustered.

Carmen interjected, "Can you tell us about her qualifications, Joel?"

"Lucy Yip taught us all here. She was the head of the Information Technology diploma program at New York University.""

"Thanks, I'll look into her background," Carmen stated.

Back in Bulldog's office, his frustration was palpable. "Something about this doesn't sit right with me," he grumbled.

"What's bothering you, mate?" I inquired.

"It's this feeling ... jobs for the boys, her actual qualifications ... Damn techies! I hope Carmen's trip here isn't for naught."

"There's still the case to crack, mate. We need to delve into the pussy app to find a lead on the murderer. Carmen's expertise will be crucial for that."

"Alright, let's get to it," Bulldog acquiesced. "Oh here ... Carmen, you might be able to use this."

He handed over Dwip's phone.

We left NYPD and headed for my office.

CHAPTER FIVE

As we approached the office door Carmen noted, "Hey, where's the sign?"

"Haven't had time to scratch myself since returning from the Yucatan," I admitted.

Carmen took a seat opposite me.

"You need to bring Patricia here to run the office," Carmen stated. "Promote Kendy to take on the smaller jobs and to get a PI license, and to do all your running around."

"It's obvious why Charlie's so efficient," I quipped.

Carmen smiled smugly, "You bet your life. So, how about you start unravelling this murder while I examine the pussy app and investigate Lucy Yip?"

"You can use Kendy's terminal. Make yourself at home, kiddo."

I phoned Kendy to check in. "Hey Kendy, how are you guys doing?"

"Pretty good, boss. We've written a couple of songs..."

"What's that... 'we've'?"

"Yeah, they liked my contribution so much they've offered me to replace Dwip."

"I didn't know you played keys?"

"I taught Dwip. I was originally meant to be the keyboard player, but then the baby came along, so..."

"What was your response?"

"I said I'd discuss it with you first."

"Will it interfere with your work?" I inquired.

"Can't see how it would."

"Then there's nothing to talk about, mate. We can work around that."

"That's so cool, boss."

"It aligns well with what Carmen suggested," I said.

"What's that?"

"Bringing Patricia here to run the office. You'd start on some smaller cases in the field while studying for your PI licence. I'll give you a reference."

"Oh man, that's amazing. Can't wait to tell the others. Give Carmen a massive hug for me."

"Enzo Cipriani is working for the LA office," I added.

"That's cool. I liked talking to him. Seems a nice guy."

"Right, so I've done some digging on Dwip, or Sonoko..."

"She hated that name..."

"Have you met her brother?"

"Ren? Yeah, he's trouble. Into drugs even after his brother Hero's overdose. Hero was a nice guy."

"Tell me about Hero."

"He got mixed up with a bad crowd. Met a woman through Dwip. Dwip regretted introducing them; Ren never forgave her. Hero became the family's patriarch after their parents' death. It's a Japanese cultural thing."

"And the woman?"

"She was Dwip's Uni teacher, Lucy Yip."

Alarm bells rang in my head. "I can't believe this. Too many coincidences."

"Why?"

"I met her at NYPD today! She was consulting on the pussy app."

"Oh my god! She's trouble. A fanatical fan who originally financed the band, had a thing with Zola, which she said felt like assault. She also tried it on with Dwip. It rumoured her actions drove Hero to his

OD. We all think she's the inspiration behind 'Femme Fatale.'"

"Unbelievable. Carmen's investigating her right now."

"Tell her to be careful. Lucy's dangerous."

"Did the phones arrive?"

"Yep. Devon's glued to his."

"How can we confirm Dwip wrote 'Femme Fatale'?"

"Check with BMI or ASCAP. They're performance rights organisations. She would've registered it with one of them."

"How do I do that?"

"Get Carmen onto it."

"Lastly, do you have a contact for Ren?"

"It's in Dwip's phone."

After hanging up with Kendy, I shared everything with Carmen. We located Ren's contact information in Dwip's phone, and Carmen agreed to call Lucy Yip under the guise of NYPD IT work to glean more information. My next step was to track down Ren.

~ ~ ~

The autopsy results that Book had texted me were disturbing. Dwip had been killed with venom from Crotalus adamanteus: the Eastern Diamondback Rattlesnake. This venom's potent hemotoxin wreaks havoc on the body by destroying red blood cells, disrupting blood clotting, and causing extensive tissue and organ damage. Notably, the point of injection was identified as her labia majora, a detail that added a chilling dimension to the case.

I showed the text to Carmen.

"Where would someone even get venom from a rattlesnake?" Carmen questioned.

"A reptile park, a zoo, an antivenom lab, or possibly a university research centre. Once we confirm the species, I'll look into it. However, I've been told toxicology reports can take up to a month."

"I left a message for Yip; we'll see if she responds," Carmen informed me.

I then called Kendy to relay the grim news. With the case now officially classified as a murder investigation, Bulldog would require them all back in town for questioning. Kendy was relieved in one sense but also anxious, knowing the killer was still at large.

Just as I ended the call with Kendy, Bulldog phoned. He was surprised I received the autopsy report before him but confirmed the shift to a murder investigation. He proposed a meeting to discuss suspects, and I invited him to the office. Things were quickly escalating. I pulled out the whiteboard to start a murder board but realised I was out of wet-erase markers.

"I need to run to the stationery shop, back in five," I called out to Carmen.

While on the street, I received a call from BMI. It was the last hope of confirming Dwip's registration of 'Femme Fatale,' but like the others, they reported no record of it. This was a major setback for the band, as they now had no way to prove the song was their original composition. However, the BMI representative offered a glimmer of hope. He suggested that if we could find recognisable components of the song's composition, such as lyrics or tape recordings, typically stored as files on a computer nowadays, we could establish copyright. I quickly phoned Kendy with this information. She agreed to stop by Dwip's apartment on her way to our office to retrieve Dwip's laptop.

~ ~ ~

I returned to the office with markers and half a dozen fresh croissants, unable to resist the lure of the French bakery.

Carmen and Bulldog, who was already there, seemed impressed. "You were quick," I remarked to Bulldog.

"I called you from the car. Carmen just made me a coffee, and you've brought croissants. No chocolate donuts?" he joked.

"Don't give him any ideas, Bulldog. He's notorious for devouring croissants," Carmen warned playfully.

"Kendy will be here soon, so we've saved one for her," I noted.

"That leaves two extras..." Carmen observed, one beautifully laminated eyebrow arched.

"Contingency," I explained.

As we enjoyed our croissants and coffee, I updated Bulldog on everything we knew, including the copyright issue with 'Femme Fatale.' We began jotting down notes on the murder board. Our leads were scarce, with Lucy Yip as our primary person of interest and Ren Tanaka on the list for an interview. Bulldog shared a more detailed autopsy report. The estimated time of death was between 1:30 AM and 7 AM, when Zola arrived. Dwip had bruises consistent with blunt-force trauma and a fall.

We theorised Dwip was attacked upon entering her apartment, knocked unconscious, and dragged inside. Her roadcase was left in the living room, and she was seated on the bathroom toilet. Her labia was injected with venom, which paralysed her respiratory system. Her shoe and sock were oddly placed in the bedroom, possibly to mislead investigators. There were no signs of regurgitation, suggesting she never regained consciousness from being knocked out. The crime scene was meticulously arranged. No fingerprints or fibres were found, indicating the perpetrator likely wore gloves and a hair covering, possibly a balaclava. There was no evidence of rape or sexual activity, and her stomach contents were normal.

"Do you think there's a direct correlation between the pussy app logo, the Yoni flower that imitates the labia, and the injection zone?" I mused.

"Perhaps," Bulldog stated. "Whoever's behind the app could the murderer."

"I'd like to know how many people it would take to make that app. Is it a one-person operation?" Carmen wondered.

"And what's the motive for killing Dwip? Is it the song?" I questioned.

"It's raking in a fortune. Too bad it's in crypto, making it untraceable," Bulldog remarked.

"For me, the key question is: if Dwip didn't compose 'Femme Fatale,' who did? It must be the murderer. The song isn't officially registered anywhere, and that's probably intentional, to avoid any leads," I concluded.

~ ~ ~

Kendy hesitated at the entrance to Dwip's apartment, uneasy about going alone, so Zola joined her. Aware that forensics would soon return for a more thorough examination, now that it was officially a crime scene, they needed to retrieve the laptop quickly and leave without a trace.

Zola waited by the roadcase while Kendy slipped into the room set up as a small recording studio. She found the laptop, disconnected it, and as she returned to the living room, she was startled to find a person clad in black, wearing a balaclava, leaning over an unconscious Zola on the floor, syringe in hand. Reacting instinctively, Kendy hurled the laptop at the assailant. It struck the arm holding the syringe, sending it flying. The attacker, clutching their injured shoulder, bolted out the door. Kendy rushed to Zola's side, lifting her head and trying to rouse her. She noticed blood on her palm; Zola had a bleeding wound on the back of her head. In desperation, Kendy called me.

I arrived with Carmen and Bulldog. Kendy, visibly relieved, broke into tears when Carmen comforted her. I was about to collect the laptop and syringe when Bulldog intervened.

"No, Axis, that's evidence. We need to cordon off the area for CSI," he said, pulling out his phone to call headquarters.

"But the analysis will take ages..." I protested.

"It doesn't matter..." Bulldog interrupted, speaking into his phone, "Request for backup and paramedics, 10-10..." He stepped outside to provide more details.

I joined Carmen and a distressed Kendy. "You alright, kiddo?" She nodded, still clinging to Carmen. Zola began to stir. "She's coming to," I said, kneeling beside her. "It's Axis, Zola. Just stay still and try to stay calm. You're safe now."

"What did you see, Kendy?" Carmen inquired gently.

"I came out with the laptop, and this person in a hoodie was about to inject Bla. I threw the laptop at the needle. Missed it, but hit the shoulder, and they ran off."

"You're sure it was a man?"

"It all happened so fast, I'm not sure. Wasn't tall ... wearing black latex gloves, and a black balaclava. Is Zola..."

"She'll be okay," I reassured her.

"He was just about to inject her..." Kendy added, her voice tremulous.

"Lucky you intervened, Kendy. You probably saved her life," Carmen said, comforting her.

~ ~ ~

We had barely settled back into the office when Carmen received a text. It was a message to meet Lucy Yip at the MO Lounge of the Mandarin Oriental Hotel at 4 PM. Carmen found the choice of location intriguing, given their shared Chinese heritage.

"Yip would have certainly done her homework on you," I remarked.

"She might have learned that the Chinese character in my name means 'why?' and is linked to the sage king Emperor Shun. She'd also find out about my master's degrees in communications and forensic criminal psychology," Carmen reflected.

"I've met her and never warmed to her, possibly due to her dealings with Dwip, Hero, and the band. Like I mentioned before, Axis, we think 'Femme Fatale' is about her. She'll likely see you as a challenge, Carmen," Kendy contributed.

"There's only two hours before your meeting, Carmen," I noted. "Let's go over the latest developments. We can assume the assailant wanted something from Dwip's apartment, probably the laptop, right?"

"If the assailant is behind the pussy app and the rip-off version of 'Femme Fatale,' then obtaining all of Dwip's song components to destroy them would fit the MO," Kendy explained.

"Do you think the assailant could be Lucy Yip, Kendy?" Carmen asked.

After a moment's contemplation, Kendy responded, "Honestly, it's hard to say for sure. The figure seemed feminine, even the movements, but I can't see Lucy Yip as the burglar type. She's cunning, sure, but not in that way."

The unmistakable ringtone of The Terrible Tango interrupted our conversation. It was Bulldog. I answered, "What's up?"

"You're not going to believe this..."

"Try me. Right now, I'm willing to believe nearly anything."

"The substance in the syringe was H2O."

"Water?" I relayed this to Kendy and Carmen, who were visibly astonished. "Bulldog says the syringe contained water." I put him on speaker so they could all hear. "Anything else I shouldn't believe?"

"There's a software program called Logic on the laptop that might contain the files Kendy mentioned."

"That's the one," Kendy called out.

"Nothing else notable. Zola will stay in the hospital overnight for concussion observation, but otherwise she's fine."

"Carmen has a meeting with Lucy Yip at 4 PM," I said.

"Do we think Yip could be our assailant?" Bulldog asked.

"We haven't ruled her out," I replied.

"Okay. With the other band members back, I'll need to speak with them. Kendy, can you arrange for them to come in?"

"Tomorrow morning at eleven?" Kendy suggested.

"Perfect. Axis, keep me updated on Carmen's meeting. Any leads on Ren Tanaka?"

"Just left a message on his phone. We'll keep trying."

"Alright, keep me in the loop."

Kendy was busy on her phone using a tracker. "Got him. Ren's at On the Rocks bar in Hell's Kitchen."

"Okay, Kendy, you're with me. Carmen, you know where the Mandarin Oriental is?"

"If I can't find it, the taxi will," she said, checking her phone.

We split up, Kendy and I heading to Hell's Kitchen and Carmen to Columbus Circle in downtown New York.

CHAPTER SIX

Charlie watched as the striking young woman, Serine Sun, approached with the confident stride of a prized filly. Her long, blonde, curled hair bounced in harmony with her perfectly sculpted figure. She could have easily been a successful model but had chosen acting instead. Her allure was undeniable, but her attitude was enough for Charlie to harbour a strong dislike, despite her being his client. He stood up as she neared the table.

"Charlie darling," Serine cooed with a feigned European kiss that didn't actually touch his cheeks. Once seated, Charlie followed suit.

"You look more beautiful every time I see you," he complimented, masking his true feelings expertly.

"I can't stay long, Charlie. There's a limo waiting to take me to the studio," Serine said, her demeanour reminiscent of Marilyn Monroe in 'Some Like It Hot.'

"Okay. I didn't want to discuss this over the phone. We need to draw out the blackmailer. He's not a professional, which is both a good and bad thing. He could be unpredictable," Charlie explained.

"So, what's the plan?" she asked, her lips forming a pout.

"We'll offer to pay the ransom in exchange for the original video."

"But what if he has copies?"

"That's a valid concern. I'll threaten to take him down if he double-crosses us."

"Oh," Serine replied, her eyes widening with a mix of surprise and intrigue. "He's asking for a hundred thousand dollars."

"Yes. Do you have it?"

"Not exactly. But I have a friend who will loan it to me."

"Great. Get the money to me by 7 PM tonight. Your friend shouldn't worry; we won't lose it. We need to act quickly, give the blackmailer no time to reconsider."

Checking her phone, Serine stood up, shedding her Marilyn persona. "That doesn't leave much time, but okay. I need this over and done with."

"I'll make the arrangements. There's no turning back now. We'll likely only have one chance at this."

She nodded and swiftly left the restaurant, her earlier glamourous demeanour replaced by a sense of urgency.

Charlie reclined in his chair and dialled his phone. "Set up the exchange for 9 PM, just as we planned ... Yeah, a real pro would've demanded at least half a million. Thanks, Enzo."

~ ~ ~

Later in the day, while at his desk in the office, Charlie heard voices at reception. Moments later, Enzo, clad in leather and sporting wraparound sunglasses, sauntered in and pulled up a chair across from Charlie. Removing his sunglasses, he grumbled, "We've hit a snag."

"He's getting cold feet?" Charlie inquired.

"No, he wants the ransom in crypto. Sent me all the details."

Charlie peered at Enzo with a hint of dismay. "So much for being an amateur."

"I reckon he's consulting with someone. There's a delay in his responses, as if he's in a different time zone. And the guy's spelling is atrocious. Look," Enzo displayed a text message on his phone, where 'crypto' was misspelled as 'criptoe'.

Charlie let out a chuckle. "Maybe he's still in kindergarten." He leaned back, contemplating their next move. "Fancy a coffee?"

"Got anything stronger?"

"Carol, bring the rye and glasses, please!" Charlie called out.

Deep in thought, they were interrupted when Carol arrived, placing the glasses on the desk and pouring a generous serving into each. Enzo's gaze lingered on her long, shapely legs.

"Leave the bottle, Carol," Charlie instructed.

Carol cast an alluring glance at Enzo as she returned to reception.

Quietly, Charlie whispered, "I think she's taken a shine to you. She's single, recently split from a long-time boyfriend, a Hell's Angel, if I recall."

"That's hardly a glowing endorsement," Enzo remarked dryly.

"Right, the Mongols and Angels aren't exactly buddies, are they?"

"Let's stay on track," Enzo suggested, steering the conversation back. "What are we going to do about this Jason Collins character?"

~ ~ ~

Carmen was enjoying the magnificent view of New York City from her window seat in the MO Lounge on the 35th floor of the Mandarin Oriental Hotel when she heard a female voice speaking Mandarin.

"Nǐ hǎo, nǐ shì Hú xiǎojiě ma?"

Looking up, Carmen saw a stylishly dressed Chinese woman in her mid-thirties. "Yes, I am Miss Hu. And you must be Miss Yip. Please, have a seat. Would you like an aperitif?"

"I think tea would be more appropriate," Yip replied.

Carmen signalled a waiter and tapped two fingers on the table, a gesture he recognised as a request for tea. Yip noticed the cultural nuance.

"You've been in the States as long as I have," Yip observed, her English polished and clear.

"A little research goes a long way, Miss Yip," Carmen replied.

"Let's drop the formalities. Call me Lucy or Yipster, as my students do."

"You're still teaching? I thought your contract with the NYPD indicated a shift to commercial projects," Carmen inquired.

"That short contract? It was just a consulting gig. I still teach part-time, allowing me to pursue other interests," Yip explained as the waiter poured Jasmine tea into their cups.

Carmen studied Yip carefully, sensing a sharp, possibly cunning personality beneath her composed exterior.

"I'm here to discuss the pussy app. Bulldog's team couldn't provide much insight, so I've been brought in from LA. It's a sophisticated piece of work," Carmen mentioned.

"It certainly is," Yip agreed. "But I was only asked about its mechanics, not how to stop it."

"But wasn't stopping it part of your brief?" Carmen pressed.

"Mr Stone might have asked, but he doesn't officially represent the NYPD."

Carmen shifted gears. "Could a single individual have created the app?"

"It's possible. Are you suggesting a larger group might be involved?"

"No, but the app seems designed for both chaos and profit from a stolen song."

"It's more complex than that. It's a brilliant digital construct, likely the work of one person."

"And probably female?"

"Perhaps. Are you insinuating I'm involved?"

"Just speculating. How can we trace the creator through the app?"

"Is the app illegal?"

"It was used in a murder, and it's generating illicit crypto revenue from 'Femme Fatale,' a song by The Lunatic Fringe. It's rumoured the song is about you, and its composer, Sonoko Tanaka, was the murder victim."

Yip's demeanour changed visibly. Standing up, she snapped, "I find your questions offensive." With that, she stormed out.

A smirk crossed Carmen's face, confident she had rattled Yip, revealing a fissure in her otherwise icy demeanour.

~ ~ ~

Kendy and I entered On the Rocks Bar in Hell's Kitchen, a quintessential small New York establishment with a few patrons scattered along the bar. The wall behind the bartender displayed an impressive array of backlit whiskey bottles from around the world, the bar's specialty. Kendy immediately spotted Ren at the far end of the bar, lost in contemplation over an empty glass.

"Ren, drowning your sorrows again?" Kendy approached him.

Ren didn't look up. "Fuck off, Ken."

I stepped in, "That's no way to talk to a lady."

He scoffed, "Didn't realise I was speaking to one. And who the fuck are you?"

"A guy you don't want to upset. We need to talk."

"Fuck off," he slurred, turning to the bartender. "Another Scotch."

The bartender exchanged a glance with me and shook his head at Ren. "I think you've had enough, fella."

"Do your job and pour," Ren demanded, his voice rising.

Before the situation escalated, I confronted Ren. "Just take a deep breath..."

He swung at me, landing a punch on my chin. It was a decent hit, but I wasn't fazed. Grabbing him firmly, I gave him a look that said, 'I could take you down if I wanted to,' and asked, "You sure you want to do this?"

He backed off, and I gestured to the bartender before guiding Ren to a booth. Kendy and I sat across from him.

"Why so down, Ren?" Kendy asked softly.

"I don't know ... When I heard about Dwip, I just..." His voice trailed off, choked with emotion.

Kendy, ever empathetic, reached out and held his hand. "I'm glad you cared enough to come for your sister."

I observed him carefully, not entirely convinced by his show of emotion. It felt like subpar acting to me. Kendy's demeanour suddenly shifted. She released Ren's hand and snapped, "Cut the bullshit, Ren. You and I both know what Dwip thought of you. Why are you really here? She was murdered, Ren..."

His feigned drunkenness seemed to dissipate. "What?"

"You heard her," I said firmly. "Your sister was murdered. How long have you been in town?"

"What, you think I had something to do with it? I might have hated her, but I wouldn't—"

"Just answer the question," I interjected sternly.

"I arrived yesterday."

"For what reason?"

"Rag Doll texted me about Dwip. I thought, being her only relative..."

"You thought there might be some money in it, right?" Kendy accused, her temper rising.

Ren stood abruptly, shooting us a venomous look before storming out of the bar. Kendy turned to me, frustration etched on her face. "Rag Doll didn't text him. He's lying. What do you think?"

"He's definitely a suspect now," I concluded. "He may not have committed the murder himself, but he could be involved somehow."

~ ~ ~

The pussy app continued to trend virally despite numerous warnings about its security. Millions who had downloaded it before telecom servers successfully filtered it were captivated. The latest craze was 'ask me who you are.' Users input their names into the AI chat feature and received astonishing insights, drawn from data aggregated across social media, search engines, and government databases in the digital metaverse. The app also offered a feature to delete this data, causing data collection agencies to scramble. Amidst this chaos, it prompted users to purchase 'Femme Fatale' to support its 'community services.' Its rebellious nature, reminiscent of WikiLeaks, resonated with a public tired of data mining and distrustful of governments. For governments, however, the app was stoking insurrection.

~ ~ ~

Professor Lucy Yip's former student, Niha Yang, had risen rapidly at the university, quickly securing a position at the pharmaceutical giant, BioBot Industries. This was part of Yip's plan: gaining access to a major public company. This partnership started two years ago, during Yip's relationship with Hero Tanaka.

Yang, eager to support her mentor, shared the nanobot technology she and Yip were developing. BioBot was so impressed they proposed buying a sixty percent stake for $100 million. All Yip needed to do was provide a working prototype.

These non-invasive nanobots, designed for intravenous injection, could target specific DNA strands and remain dormant until activated remotely via 5G. They had the potential to transmute and mimic virtually any cellular substance.

Working alongside Yip, Yang stood to earn a significant portion of the $100 million if BioBot decided to invest. This opportunity hinged on their ability to bring the nanobot technology to fruition.

~ ~ ~

Still seething from her intense encounter with Carmen, Yip stormed back into her office to find Niha Yang engrossed in work at her computer. Yang, standing at 5' 7", matched Yip in height but not in appearance. Unlike the more traditionally attractive Yip, Yang had transformed her once slight frame into a robust one through diligent gym workouts and martial arts training. Her admiration for Yip was more than professional—it was romantic, though unreciprocated. Nevertheless, Yang held on to a glimmer of hope for a deeper relationship.

Yip, barely containing her anger, started furiously inputting data into her computer.

Sensing Yip's frustration, Yang ventured cautiously, "The meeting didn't go well, I take it?"

Yip took a deep breath and swivelled to face Yang. "That's

putting it mildly. It was an absolute setup. She was fishing for personal information. I need to find out who's behind this Carmen Hu."

"Hu? Isn't that the Chinese character for tiger? A formidable opponent," Yang remarked.

"I don't care about that nonsense," Yip retorted, returning her focus to the computer. She quickly found a connection. "Look at this. Axis Stone heads the New York office of Stone, Vargas, and Chan Investigations. They don't have a website, but I found a photo of Stone with Kendy Lee as his PA. Interesting ... What's their link to Carmen Hu, I wonder?"

Their conversation was interrupted by Yang's notification tone. "I just received an email from Dixon at BioBot. They want the working model for their AGM in 30 days."

Yip, overwhelmed, buried her face in her hands. "Great, a deadline on top of everything else."

"Don't worry, we're on track with our development schedule," Yang reassured her confidently.

~ ~ ~

Carmen breezed into the office, finding Kendy and me at our computers. I left my desk to join Carmen on the sofa, with Kendy following close behind, eager to hear about Carmen's meeting.

Carmen started, "Yip's a tough nut to crack. But I managed to rattle her when I raised the issue of 'Femme Fatale' being about her. She didn't take it well and stormed out. She doesn't seem to like you much, Axis."

"How odd, the opposite sex usually finds me appealing ... There must be something seriously wrong with her taste," I half-joked.

"Like the song says, she's only interested in what she can gain," Kendy added.

"Did you catch up with Ren Tanaka?" Carmen inquired.

"We had a similar experience," Kendy replied. "He freaked out and left when we pressed him about why he's here."

"A few years back in Sydney, I had a collie/kelpie cross puppy. I bought him from a farmer a couple of hundred clicks out of Sydney. The little fella was the last in the litter, and when he saw me, he rolled over onto his back, showing off his pink belly. He was telling me his name was Floyd."

Carmen looked puzzled until Kendy explained, "Pink Floyd, his favourite band."

"So, I get Floyd home, and I notice he had this habit of shaking his head. The vet said it was just a habit, but later, I found out it was due to a colony of parasites in his ear. Once treated, he never shook his head again."

Kendy smiled and told Carmen, "He likes telling stories with a moral."

"The obvious isn't always the cause," I concluded. "And I think that goes for both Ren Tanaka and Professor Yip."

CHAPTER
SEVEN

After sharing my story, Carmen called Charlie to update him. Concerned about the sudden shift to a crypto ransom, Charlie asked to speak with me, recalling my expertise in handling kidnap and blackmail cases. We spent the next half hour strategizing, drawing on my experience from the Lovejoy case in Manila and incorporating Nick's successful amendment. Satisfied with the plan, Charlie ended the call.

Charlie looked at Enzo across the table. "We have a plan in place. What's our next step?"

"I need to confirm the crypto payment with him," Enzo replied.

"Make sure he understands we only pay after confirming the original video and ensuring there are no copies."

"How do we verify that?" Enzo questioned.

"He'll hand over the phone with the original video on it. Carmen is sending me instructions to check the phone if there have been copies or downloads."

"That's smart," Enzo noted.

"So, once he gives you the phone, you do the checks. If it's all clear, text me the account details he'll give you for the crypto transfer."

"And the money from Serina?"

"We'll convert it to crypto," Charlie confirmed.

"Got it," Enzo nodded.

"After you send the text and I confirm the transfer, I'll give you a code to give him. Once he has the code, he'll know the payment is complete."

"Okay…" Enzo said, looking mystified. "So, he gets away with it?"

"No, we have the cops waiting in hiding and they take it from there."

"Are they cool with that?"

"Axis is calling a mate in LAPD, who will sort it out," Charlie explained.

Enzo reclined in his chair, sort of convinced but still confused about how the money would be returned.

Before he could inquire further, Carol entered the room. "Detective Carlos Santana from the LAPD is on the line for you, Charlie."

Charlie excused himself to take the call, leaving Enzo to ponder the intricacies of their elaborate scheme.

~ ~ ~

Lucy Yip's heart raced as she read the ransom demand text: one million in crypto for a six-minute video, or it would be sent to BioBot in 10 days. The message included a compromising screenshot of her and Serina Sun. The memory of that night, only six months ago during an IT convention in LA, flooded back. She had met Serina in the hotel bar, and there had been an undeniable spark. Frantically, Lucy found Serina's number and called her.

"Hello, Serina? It's Lucy, we met…"

"I remember. Are you calling about being blackmailed?"

"Yes. Wait, you too?"

"We're making the exchange tonight," Serina revealed.

"You're paying? … How did this happen?" Lucy inquired.

"He filmed us from a security monitor. It is Hollywood, after all."

"When did he contact you?"

"About two weeks ago."

"I wonder why he waited so long," Lucy pondered aloud.

"He probably found out about my forthcoming role in a big studio movie. Bad press now would ruin me."

"That's awful."

"I'm paying a hundred thousand," Serina said, sounding defeated.

"Only that? I've been asked for a million!"

"What! Why so much?"

"I'm about to close a hundred-million-dollar deal. The blackmailers must know."

"How?"

"I have no idea. But if that video leaks, I'll lose everything."

"Do you have that kind of money?" Serina inquired.

"I could get it, but there's no guarantee it'll stop there. They're offering us each a copy of the video, so that's an admission there are at least two copies in existence."

"You're right. You should talk to my PI, Charlie Chan. He's handling the case."

"Is he in LA? I'm in New York."

"I think he has an office there. Let me get you his number."

The moment Serina mentioned Stone, Vargas and Chan Investigations, Lucy felt a wave of disbelief wash over her.

"I've sent you the number. Lucy, you still there?"

"Yes, yes, sorry, just checking the text," Lucy lied, her mind reeling from the connections—Kendy, Axis Stone, Chan, Carmen Hu. Contacting them was out of the question, especially after her conversation with Serina. Overwhelmed, she sank deeper into her chair, trying to fathom a way out of the intricate web in which she had become entangled.

~ ~ ~

Serina promptly reached out to Charlie regarding her encounter with Lucy Yip. Charlie, already entangled in the web of connections involving Carmen, myself, and Yip, was now deeply concerned about the existence of two separate videos and potentially two blackmailers.

After pondering the situation, Charlie deduced that the blackmailers must be in cahoots.

Meanwhile, Enzo had just dismounted his chopper when his phone buzzed. "Charlie, what's up?" he answered.

Charlie quickly briefed Enzo on the latest development. Enzo, equally taken aback, pondered aloud, "They've got to be connected, but why would one settle for a hundred grand when the other's aiming for a mill? If you can make a million, why bother with a hundred?"

"You'll need to tell him we're aware of the second video. How can he ensure his partner isn't duplicating more copies?" Charlie posed.

"I think they each have their own target," Enzo speculated. "They're working independently, but one or both must have known about the other woman."

"Exactly. Our blackmailer likely knew it was Serina, while the other knew about Yip. He's supposed to call me in five minutes. He keeps it brief, probably scared of being traced," Enzo said.

"Where are you now?"

"Just grabbed a burger. I'll call you back with any new info. You have the ransom ready?"

"Serina's having it transferred," Charlie confirmed.

~ ~ ~

Once a fool always a fool I'm told
After the show, aficionado.
Hangout man, your backstage plans are cold
Openings unfold, aficionado.

I've had it up to here
You thought that you had me
You didn't see the tear fall
Fall as you left me
Well, I don't want to know, know, know, aficionado
I don't want to know, know, know, aficionado

I've had it up to here
With all the games
You dressing-room lovers
Drive me insane

I don't want to know, know, know, aficionado
I don't want to know, know, know, aficionado

You made me your fool
That's your golden rule
You told me to quit
So I held on a little bit
Arrr-har!
I see you lying there
With your iron eyes
I feel you choking me
Femme fatale surprise
Arrr-har!

I don't want to know, know, know, aficionado
I don't want to know, know, know, aficionado

The gig was packed to the rafters. The audience gave The Lunatic Fringe a standing ovation, not that anyone was seated; they had all been up dancing their faces off. The band headed for the dressing room. It had been Kendy's first time performing live on keys. Devon greeted the girls in the dressing room.

"Great job, girls. Kendy, you were fantastic."

"Just wish we were making money out of the song," Rag Doll complained bitterly.

Slick was packing her Fender Stratocaster away. "Yeah, what's with that new thing on the app? Have you seen it?"

"Yeah, it's getting tons of press, more downloads," Butch lamented.

"Don't worry, girls. While Ken's got her super-sleuth boss on the case, we're in with a chance at the big bucks, isn't that right, Ken?" Zola said.

"He's pretty sharp," Kendy replied.

"That's more than I can say for our new manager here," Rag grumbled.

Devon pointed at himself in shock. "What, moi? Hey, I inherited this mess, don't blame me."

"Don't worry, Dev. That's what managers are for—gotta have someone to whinge at, right, girls?" Zola said with a chuckle.

Kendy asked Zola quietly, "Have you had any more threats?"

"No, nothing since that first one. Maybe after the attack, he's given up on us."

Kendy then asked, "Are you still using the app, Rag?"

As Rag Doll looked in the mirror and began removing her makeup, she admitted, "I check it every now and then, mainly to see how many downloads the song's getting." She undid her shirt, ready to change into her regular clothes.

"You're just jealous of how Pussy looks," Slick teased.

Rag Doll swivelled quickly on her chair, pulled open her shirtfront, exposing her sizable breasts, and shook them at Slick, singing jokingly, "She ain't got nothing on me, babe!"

Zola watched as Devon turned away. "What's wrong, Dev? Don't you like titties?"

All the girls laughed as Devon blushed.

~ ~ ~

Yang was at her computer, closely watching Lucy, who was pacing the office anxiously, chewing on her knuckle. They were both waiting for the next text from the blackmailer. In preparation, Yang had routed Yip's phone through her computer to facilitate their plan.

As the text arrived, Lucy leaned over Yang's shoulder to read the message on the screen. It read: "confirm by return text you can make the exchange—no cops—no-one or BioBot gets the video." Without hesitation, Yang typed 'yes' and hit send.

This response carried a secret weapon—a bot embedded in the data. This bot, a product of their development, would infiltrate the sender's phone and send back a programmed GPS ping to Lucy's phone every 15 minutes. Remarkably, the bot's design allowed it to function regardless of whether the phone was on or off or the number was blocked.

Yang looked up at Lucy, a hint of triumph in her expression. "Done."

"We will need to work fast in case he trashes the phone," Lucy commented, still pacing.

"Leave it to me," Yang replied confidently.

Lucy was content to do that; she had more pressing matters to consider, with the looming deadline to present to BioBot drawing near.

~ ~ ~

Dressed in a pink robe and slippers, Jason Collins sat nervously in his small Santa Monica bedsit, blinds drawn, feeling out of his element. Blackmailing wasn't his forte; he was only involved to appease Ren. Their relationship hinged on these whims, and this time it had escalated to blackmailing two women. What started as a joke with a video had turned into a serious, unsettling crime.

As the time to text arrived, Jason swallowed his fear and sent the pre-prepared text, then waited anxiously for a response.

The reply was unexpected and unnerving: "I will only pay once you surrender your phone with the original video on it. Confirm it is the only copy. What about the copy in New York?"

Panic surged through him. "How do they know about that?" he muttered, heart racing.

Frantically, he called Ren. "They know about you ... The guy I'm dealing with wants proof there's only one video. They even mentioned the video you have. Yes, they know, Ren. Yes, I'm worried. Okay, okay, I'll try that. I love you."

He typed another text; "Once the deal is done, there will be no more demands on Miss Sun. If you don't comply, I will send the video to the studio."

Enzo was sitting side-saddle on his bike in the car park of a Santa Monica liquor store, reading the text from Jason. The sun was setting. He phoned Charlie. "Hey Charlie, he took the bait, are you ready? Okay."

He sent the final text and waited for a reply. It came quickly, "V tree, Goose Egg Park, 7.30. I'll be carrying a red shoulder bag." It was just past seven, and Goose Egg Park wasn't far from him. He texted the location and time to Charlie, then started up his chopper.

If he had been nervous before, now Jason was close to panic. He quickly erased everything on his phone but the original video in the phone memory, removed the SIM, and snapped it in half. In a flap, he rushed into the bedroom to change.

Enzo stepped off his bike on 7th Street; it would only take a couple of minutes to walk from there to Goose Egg Park. It was a pleasant evening, with a few people walking their dogs and exercising. In his leathers, he looked a little out of place on the footpath, being passed by sweating joggers. It wasn't often he paid attention to the sounds surrounding him—his own boot steps, car horns, sirens, barking dogs, planes flying over, waves lapping on Santa Monica beach, all mixed with the general humdrum of urban life. Then he heard the sound of sneakers slapping concrete approaching from behind. To avoid confusion on the footpath, he walked a straight line, keeping left, but many joggers coming towards him were wearing headphones and seemed lost in their athletic daze, forcing them to dodge him last minute.

After a few minutes of annoyance, he chose to ignore the path and cut through the park. It was a small egg-shaped park, and he soon sighted the rendezvous point—a massive V-shaped tree. He slowed and checked the time on his phone; he was 5 minutes early. He reached the tree and leaned his back against the huge trunk, with a clear view of the footpaths.

In the last few minutes, there seemed to be fewer people in and around the park, probably due to the darkness or dinner time. Then he noticed a person walking along the path with a red shoulder bag. He wasn't expecting a woman. As the person neared, he could make out that she was tall, thin, bespectacled, with blonde hair worn up and wrapped in a colourful scarf. She was wearing a dark blue cardigan over a white blouse, a knee-length brown skirt, and sneakers. When she reached him and stopped, he realised that she was actually a man in drag. He looked as surprised to meet a Mongol biker in leathers as Enzo was to meet him.

Without uttering a word, the person took the phone from her red bag and handed it to Enzo. He opened the phone at the video and keyed in a simple code Charlie had given him. It showed that there had been 2 copies of the video produced and no downloads. It also showed that it had been played sixteen times.

"There have been two copies of the video," Enzo said gruffly. He could tell she was reluctant to talk and was very nervous.

She coughed and then muttered in a disguised voice, "One copy was sent to Serina, and the one in New York, you know about."

Enzo nodded; it added up. The video file name had the bank account number. He entered the numbers on his phone and sent it as a text.

It only took seconds, but as the two of them stood in silence waiting for a reply, for Jason, it felt like it was taking ages. Then Enzo's phone sounded a text alert. He showed his phone to Jason. On the screen was a confirmation code. Jason took a notepad and pen from his bag, jotted it down, turned, and moved quickly away.

~ ~ ~

Jason entered his apartment and flopped onto the sofa, his heart rate returning to normal. He smiled to himself. It had worked. Ren was right; he just needed to keep the faith. As he closed his eyes and took a deep, relaxing breath, the door burst open. Cops stormed in, guns drawn, and shouting commands. In seconds, Jason was on the floor, hands behind his head, trembling with fear. Standing in the doorway were Detective Carlos Santana, Charlie, and Enzo. The job was done.

As Charlie, Carlos, and Enzo walked towards their vehicles, Charlie, looking puzzled at Jason's appearance, asked Enzo, "Are we sure we got the right person?"

"Yeah, wasn't expecting Little Red Riding Hood, though," Enzo replied with a hint of amusement.

Carlos, joining in the conversation, remarked, "He obviously hadn't thought this through. Now he's looking at doing time. You mentioned Axis is dealing with a bigger drama involving the same video?"

They paused beside Santana's SUV. "Good work, Enzo. We'll press Jason for his accomplice's identity in New York. That should assist Axis. Is Bulldog involved?"

"He is. You know him?" Charlie inquired.

"Yeah, he's a solid cop. He and Axis work well together. And congrats on the new venture with Nick. It's a good setup," Carlos complimented.

After exchanging handshakes, Carlos drove off, leaving Charlie and Enzo watching as Jason was escorted into an LAPD car.

"So, how do we get the money back?" Enzo asked.

"What money?" Charlie responded, feigning ignorance.

"The hundred grand in crypto?"

Charlie gestured towards Enzo's chopper. Enzo nodded, and Charlie climbed on, gripping the handlebars on the extended forks—he looked totally out of place. Charlie explained, "The money went from Serina's backer to my account. I bought $100,000 worth of Ripple XRP crypto, then transferred 50 Ripple XRP to Jason's account."

"So, like forty bucks?" Enzo asked, catching on.

"Exactly. We never specified the amount, did we? Then, I sold the Ripple for a ten percent profit, returned the hundred grand to Serina's investor, and kept ten grand for us to party with—minus the forty bucks, of course."

"Axis's idea?" Enzo inquired.

"Nick's, originally. But yes, Axis put it into play."

"How did you know you'd win on the bet?"

Charlie grinned. "Chinese love a flutter."

Enzo shook his head in awe, impressed by the cunning manoeuvre.

CHAPTER
EIGHT

Ren stood in front of the bathroom mirror, examining his reflection. As a Sansei, a third-generation Japanese American, he acknowledged his handsome features. Peeling off his T-shirt, he flexed his muscles, admiring his well-maintained physique. Yet, a nagging question haunted him: "What am I doing in this dingy flophouse in the Lower East Side of Manhattan?" It was a sobering thought for someone who, not long ago, had shown great promise.

Ren had been a rising star, but he hadn't truly failed at acting; he had simply given up on it. Unlike his industrious parents and siblings, he had been the pampered youngest child, never needing to strive for anything. That all changed with the tragic car accident that claimed his parents' lives. Suddenly, he was forced to drop out of university and fend for himself, unlike his brother Hero and sister Sonoko, who had already graduated.

A chilling thought crossed his mind as he gazed into his brown, almond-shaped eyes: Could he be cursed? The fiery death of his parents, Hero's overdose, Sonoko's murder—it was a series of calamities that seemed more than just coincidence.

Shaking off the eerie feeling, Ren pulled his T-shirt back on and slumped onto the bed. It was the video featuring Professor Lucy Yip that had sparked a glimmer of hope in him. Perhaps this was the turning point he had been waiting for, his chance to alter the course of his dwindling fortunes.

At 10 PM, Ren's thoughts were dominated by a craving for sushi. He was on Bowery Street, directly opposite Chinatown. He checked a list of local restaurants and found Go Sushi a couple of blocks from the hotel.

With Jason, his partner and the main breadwinner, focusing on their elaborate blackmail scheme, Ren's financial situation was tight. The more ambitious part of their plan, orchestrated by Ren, required a significant investment, leaving him with just twenty dollars for his sushi fix. He decided on a special Maki combo for $19.95 and called to place his order for takeout.

~ ~ ~

Carmen was relieved when Charlie rang to report the blackmail case was done and dusted without casualties. She handed me the phone, "Hey Charlie, congrats on closing your first case."

"Thanks, Axis. It was a team effort. Having Santana on board really helped smooth things out."

"Carlos is a gem, no doubt about it," I agreed.

"He's confident he'll get the name of the accomplice out of Jason."

"I wouldn't expect less from him. By the way, how did your client and Yip cross paths?" I asked.

"Yip was here attending an IT convention. It finished up, and she returned to her hotel and decided on a nightcap. My client, Serina Sun, had just finished a meeting at the hotel and also went for a nightcap ... two lost souls at closing time ended up making time by the pool. Little did they know they were being watched on a security monitor. The lone security guard recognised Serina and so, just for fun, videoed the monitor with his phone. Apparently, when he showed it to his partner, he was the one who came up with the idea of blackmail, supposedly it was the partner who recognised Yip."

"Interesting," I mused.

"Yeah, and Enzo had a surprise at the exchange—the blackmailer showed up in drag."

I chuckled. "A biker and a drag queen, quite a contrast. Seems like the guy we're dealing with in Yip's case might be gay. It could be useful for profiling, though I doubt it's related to our murder case."

"It's a stretch, but worth mentioning to Bulldog. I'll keep you posted on any new developments."

After the call, I pondered the strange intersections of our cases as Carmen took back the phone.

Kendy's call from her office brought a concerning update. "The pussy app is boasting a million downloads of 'Femme Fatale.' Rag Doll's going to be fuming."

Carmen and I joined Kendy, and I suggested, "It's getting late. Let's wrap up for the day."

Reflecting on my encounter with Yip, Carmen noted, "There's a stronger connection here than what's apparent, similar to your analogy with Floyd, Axis. Yip was linked to the band, the song's about her, and she has the IT skills to create the app."

"Exactly," Kendy concurred. "And she had early access to the song, not to mention a deep resentment towards Dwip over Hero's death."

"Wondering if that resentment could lead to murder?" I pondered aloud.

Kendy weighed the thought. "Hard to say, but the motive is there. And like you always say, where there's motive, there's probability."

"You see, Kendy's learned a lot from me," I said, half-jokingly to Carmen.

Carmen agreed with Kendy's assessment. "Yip's our prime suspect. If we can link her to the app, then isn't there a copyright angle we could use?"

"But Dwip didn't register the song," I pointed out.

"Would Yip be aware of that?" Kendy asked thoughtfully.

"Are we considering a bluff?" I inquired.

"Precisely," Kendy replied. "If Yip is behind the app, she has a lot to lose if the song's copyright ownership is challenged."

I then questioned, "Did Dwip write the entire song?"

Kendy remembered, "Not entirely. We all contributed. Dwip mainly wrote the verses and the melody."

"So, it's essentially a band collaboration?" I suggested.

"Yes, like most of our work," Kendy confirmed.

We now had a potential angle, but first, we needed to substantiate it. Meanwhile, bluffing Yip could reveal her role in creating the app.

Carmen added, "Legally, copyright is established by the date of creation."

"That means we need the Logic files from Dwip's laptop," Kendy realised. "They'll have the date the song was composed."

~ ~ ~

It was 11 by the time I'd dropped Kendy and Carmen off at Kendy's apartment. With the murderer still on the loose, we needed to maintain vigilance, so walking home from the office was not an option.

I was eagerly anticipating Patricia's arrival tomorrow. She had agreed to move here for a few months to try running the office. Though she hadn't been in the workforce for a while, her exceptional organisational skills were precisely what I needed. Her presence would also allow Kendy to better apply her investigative skills and focus on her band. The added bonus for me was the prospect of having the beautiful Patricia to cuddle up to. Mixing romance and work is always tricky, but Carmen and Charlie were a fine example of making it work. As I parked my car, Santana called. "Hey Carlos, went well with Charlie, huh?"

"Yes, pretty clean, no casualties. But we couldn't get anything out of Jason Collins. He's not willing to give up his lover," Carlos informed.

"That's tough. What's next?"

"We're not done. The other blackmailer, targeting Lucy Yip in New York, falls under split jurisdiction. I'll be coordinating with Bulldog tomorrow. We also have a warrant to search Collins' apartment, which might lead us to the identity of his boyfriend."

"Thanks for the heads-up, Carlos."

"Oh by the way, I bumped into Beleza the other day, and she asked after you."

"Thanks, buddy, that's a little too distracting for right now."

"I hear you, anyways, she and little Samantha are fine. She was just wondering if you wanted that motorbike her sister Malika left you."

"If it's in the way, I'll ask Enzo to collect it; he could look after it for me."

"That'd be a wise move, by the look of his own, the dude knows his bikes."

~ ~ ~

Rag Doll called Kendy in a panic. "I've got a death threat," she said, sounding worried.

"What does it say?"

"'Stop trying to claim my song or your photo will make the headlines in a body-bag.'"

"Where are you now?" Kendy asked.

"Just about to go into Go Sushi."

"Alone?"

"No, Slick's with me. Wait, that's Dwip's brother Ren over there getting takeout."

"We met up with him earlier, low bastard. He's only here to get what he can from Dwip's estate," Kendy growled.

"Should I say hello to him?" Rag inquired.

"Yeah, why not ... he might tell you the real reason he's in town, but count your fingers, you know he's a scammer. Look, I'll let Axis know about the threat, go home and lock the door."

"Okay love. Kiss, kiss."

Kendy immediately rang to tell me about the threat on Rag Doll and her seeing Ren at Go Sushi.

"Small world Lower Manhattan. You gave her the right advice.

That threat totally links the pussy app to the murder of Dwip. I heard from Carlos in LA, he didn't get anything out of the blackmailer but he's going to search his apartment tomorrow, hopefully he'll come up with a name. Just a thought, is Ren gay?"

"He's always been a switch-hitter, but with a penchant for guys. Are you thinking what I'm thinking?" Kendy asked.

"I think so, what if Ren is the boyfriend? … it makes total sense," I said excitedly. "He would've recognised Yip in the video."

"That's it!" Kendy almost shouted. "That's why he's here; to blackmail her."

"And you know what?"

"What?"

"While he's doing that, he's helping us," I said.

"How do you work that out?"

"He's stressing her out … She must have a reason to want that video destroyed. If she's behind the pussy app, the money it's raking in would be a huge incentive," I speculated, trying to piece together the puzzle.

"But how would Ren be aware that she's involved with the app? There has to be another angle to this," Kendy pondered aloud, a hint of frustration in her voice. "Wait a second, there was something else … When Yip was with Hero, she was working on some nanobot technology. She believed it could revolutionise the world and make her a fortune. What if she's actually accomplished it?"

I was surprised. "I thought she was just an IT specialist?"

"She is, but nanobot technology essentially deals with coding. She was experimenting with code that could be integrated into a person's DNA. It would lie dormant until remotely activated for a specific purpose, like targeting cancer cells."

"Good grief, that's Nobel prize stuff."

"I know, as much as I hate her she is brilliant," Kendy admitted.

"Why would she risk all that for the app?" I questioned.

Kendy had an insight. "Maybe she needed funding for her project. Theoretical work is one thing, but a working model costs a lot."

Our conversation revealed a complex web of connections and motives. "Kendy, I think you've hit the nail on the head. This connection is the key."

Excited by her own reasoning, Kendy was taken aback. "So, what's our next move, boss?"

"I'll meet Bulldog tomorrow and see where we can go from there. Make sure Rag Doll stays safe. And when Patricia arrives, can you help her settle in?"

"Will do. Goodnight, boss."

As I ended the call, the weight of the situation became clear. Tomorrow's meeting with Bulldog would be crucial in untangling this intricate case.

~ ~ ~

Rag bumped into Ren as he was exiting Go Sushi with his takeout. "Hey, is that you, Ren Tanaka?"

Ren, caught off guard, responded, "Rag Doll, how's it going?"

"It's been a while, hasn't it?" Rag noted. "You remember Slick, right? She's with the band.

Ren gave a nod of recognition. "Yeah, hey Slick. Terrible about sis."

Rag didn't miss a beat. "You know she was murdered?"

"I heard. Met Kendy recently, and she filled me in. Who would want to kill Dwip for God's sake?"

"That's the million-dollar question. And now they're threatening Bla and me." Rag showed him the text.

Ren's expression changed. "Fuck, you serious! What are you going to do about it?"

Slick, with a hint of scepticism, asked, "What would you suggest, Ren?"

"Cops, I guess?" he replied somewhat uncertainly.

Rag shook her head. "This is the Apple; you should know it doesn't work like that unless you have influence. We're trying to figure it out ourselves. But why are you in town?"

Before Ren could answer, a couple of fans interrupted to compliment Rag. "Hey Rag Doll, looking good," one of them said.

"Thanks, man," Rag told the fan.

With the momentary distraction, Ren avoided answering the question. Rag, however, was persistent. "We've got 'Femme Fatale' out now. Remember, Dwip wrote it about Lucy Yip?"

"Did she?" Ren said, his tone growing serious. "You don't think that got her killed?"

Rag frowned. "Why would you say that?"

Ren shrugged. "Yip's always been trouble. What she did to Hero and all..."

Slick, still doubtful of Ren's intentions, pressed on. "So, really, why are you here?"

Ren sighed. "When I heard about Dwip, I wanted to pay my respects. I'm all that's left of our family."

Slick didn't buy it. "Aw, not really your style to be sentimental, Ren."

Rag, thinking on her feet, invited him, "We're heading back to my place for sushi and a smoke. You in?"

"Why not?" Ren agreed, seemingly casual about the invitation.

Rag was hoping that by having more people around it would increase their safety, given the looming threat from the murderer. As they left Go Sushi none of them paid much attention to the person in the dark hoodie standing in the shadows outside. Nor did they notice that person following them.

CHAPTER
NINE

At 2 AM, Ren rolled out of bed, his head spinning from too many vodkas and the lingering effects of ecstasy. Groggily, he glanced at the two naked women asleep together, then got dressed. He hoped the night's events would be a blur by morning, both for him and for them.

Staggering to the front door in the dim light, he managed to lock it behind him. The prospect of descending six flights of stairs was daunting, especially as he fought the urge to vomit. He hesitantly started down the dark stairway.

Only a few steps in, a dark figure burst from the shadows, brandishing a syringe. Ren reacted instantly, seizing the hand that held the syringe, struggling to keep it from his neck. It was too dark to see the assailant's face, but from the body shape, he could tell he was grappling with a woman, surprisingly strong.

With all his might, he slammed her hand against the banister, dislodging the syringe. It clattered to the floor. The brief lull in the struggle allowed him to land a punch, hitting her on the chin. She staggered, then pushed him, causing him to slip and fall on the steps.

As Ren released her, she retreated and darted down the stairs. Left blinking against the spinning room, he vomited. After a few minutes, he gathered himself, with the dizzying disorientation subsiding, he resumed his descent, eager to reach the safety of his hotel and bed.

The noise from the scuffle outside had roused Rag Doll from her sleep. Clad in a pink fluffy dressing gown and matching slippers, she grabbed a torch and cautiously opened the front door. The beam of the torch cut through the darkness of the landing as she bravely scanned the area, looking for any sign of Ren, who she realised had left.

Finding no-one in sight, her torchlight caught a glimmer on the floor. Curiosity piqued, she approached and discovered a syringe lying there. The memory of Zola's attack, also involving a syringe, flashed through her mind. With care, she picked up the syringe, realising its potential significance, and retreated back into the safety of her apartment.

~ ~ ~

Bulldog had just hung up the phone just as I flopped into the chair opposite him.

"That was your LAPD mate, Carlos Santana."

"Yeah, he said he'd call you. What did he find at the blackmailer's apartment?"

"Not much. Just a photo of Jason Collins with someone he thinks might be his partner. He's sending it over. As for Yip, I called her, but she's tight-lipped, which suggests she's being blackmailed but doesn't want it known. What's your take?"

"It's a sensitive issue," I replied, showing Bulldog the video Charlie had sent me. He watched it with a mix of intrigue and concern.

"Recognising Yip in the video suggests the blackmailer knows her well."

"That's what I thought. Kendy reckons Yip has developed an injectable nanobot that can mend things in a person's DNA."

Bulldog nodded thoughtfully. "She'd be sitting on a goldmine if that's case. That might explain why she's being blackmailed."

"Exactly, maybe so much she can't risk this video affecting it?"

"I'd say that'd be on the money. High stakes, though. Carlos was saying Jason Collins was an amateur blackmailer..."

"Yes, Charlie said the same. You'd have to imagine the same applies to his accomplice."

"That's a worry. In some ways, it's better to be dealing with a pro; amateurs can be unpredictable. You think the blackmail, Tanaka's murder, and the Pussy app are connected?" Bulldog said, reclining in his chair, causing it to protest under his bulk.

"I do. But if Yip has developed injectable nanobots and sitting on a fortune, why would she risk it all?"

I proceeded to explain all I knew and the tenuous connections between everything—even while telling him, I realised there was one vital element still missing, and Bulldog didn't waste any time in pointing it out.

"It all makes sense except you've got no proof of any of it. Is Yip the creator of the Pussy App? Is what the app doing, fraud? We know it's Yip in the blackmail video, but like I say, until she reports it, we have no case ... and we know Yip's connection to Sonoko Tanaka, but that doesn't prove she murdered her. Now, if she did, why? Like you said, why would she risk everything by murdering her and threatening others? We're missing something here."

"Everything surrounds Yip," I said, "so, if we're looking for a missing link, it's to do with her."

As we were discussing it, I received a text from Kendy. "Rag Doll just found a syringe. Ren Tanaka was attacked outside her apartment. It sounds like the same method used on Zola and possibly how Dwip was murdered."

Bulldog asked, "So, is Ren Tanaka the boyfriend blackmailer of Yip?"

I was thinking through out loud. "It would make sense that Yip would want him eliminated, and the syringe connects that with the attempt on Zola's life, and maybe how Dwip was murdered."

"Never bought the rattlesnake venom scenario," Bulldog admitted. "We'll know more soon, the tox report is due today."

"What if she used one of her nanobots to mimic rattlesnake

venom?" I mumbled.

Bulldog heard me and said, "Now you're talking."

"But the syringe that was used on Zola proved to be filled with water, what if this one's the same?"

Bulldog had a revelation. "What if it's only imitating water?"

He'd only just finished the sentence when he received a text. He checked his phone. "It's from Carlos, says, 'Sorry, it's all I could get for you, show it to Axis.'"

Looking at the photo on Bulldog's phone, I recognised one of the men. "That's Ren Tanaka."

Bulldog perked up. "This is getting more interesting by the minute. You were right, my friend."

~ ~ ~

When I arrived at the office, I walked into a lively scene. Kendy, Carmen, Patricia, Slick, and Rag Doll were all gathered for morning tea, their conversation so loud I could hear it from the ground floor.

I gave Patricia a massive bear hug, which earned applause from the rest of the ladies. As I raised my hand for quiet, the chatter subsided. "Guys, I've got some news. Carlos Santana, the LA cop, not the musician, who worked with Charlie on the Serina Sun case, sent over a photo of Jason Collins's accomplice." I held up my phone for them to see, and their reactions were of shock and recognition.

"For those who don't know, Ren Tanaka in the photo on the left, is the brother of Sonoko Tanaka, or Dwip, the victim in our murder case," I explained, especially for Carmen and Patricia.

"Far out!" Rag Doll exclaimed, handing me a syringe. "So, he's the one blackmailing Yip?"

I showed them the blackmail video, which elicited a few surprised looks. "Kendy, Bulldog, and I think this syringe contains nanobots, not just water. We believe Yip's nanobot technology, which can mimic rattlesnake venom, was used to kill Dwip."

"So, is Yip the murderer?" Kendy inquired.

"Maybe, maybe not," I responded.

"Ah, come on Axis, it has to be her," Slick interjected.

"We're not sure yet. She's potentially selling her nanobot tech for millions. Why risk that?" I posited. "It might be someone connected to her or who stands to profit from her success."

"What about the Pussy App? Is she behind that too?" Rag Doll questioned.

"We think so. It's probably funding her nanobot research," Kendy speculated.

As Slick and Rag Doll prepared to leave Rag Doll said, "Don't forget rehearsals tonight, Kendy."

"I've written a new song we could try out," Kendy said.

"What's it called?" Slick asked.

"Rita," Kendy said a little coyly.

Once Carmen, Slick, and Rag Doll had left, it was just Kendy, Patricia, and me. I found it hard to take my eyes off Patricia, who looked stunning. Carmen announced her plans to return to LA, as Charlie had a new case.

"I can drop you at JFK if you like," I offered.

"No, an Uber will do," she replied.

After farewells, the office quieted down, leaving just Kendy, Patricia, and me to discuss our next moves.

I examined the syringe closely and turned to Patricia. "Are you up to speed on everything in the office?"

Perched on the edge of my desk, Patricia pointed at her luggage. "First, where do these go?"

I grinned, "My place."

She chuckled. "And that's part of the job description?"

"Absolutely. Just ask Carmen, she's well-versed in the conditions of employment," I said jokingly.

Patricia then pointed out something missing in our office setup.

"Where's the reception area?" she asked, drawing Kendy's attention. "This place requires a serious makeover."

I opened my desk drawer, took out a key, got up chuckling, and walked Patricia into Kendy's room, then up to a door. I opened it, reached in, and flicked on the light.

"My dad's private study in situ."

Inside I felt a wave of nostalgia. "I've not entered here since he passed," I confessed to Patricia and Kendy. "It's been kept this way for sentimental reasons, but it's time to move on."

Kendy joined Patricia and me at the doorway, peering into the room. It was bland but larger than the other offices. The furniture was minimal: a small writing desk with a dusty old chair behind it, a maroon leather armchair in one corner next to a reading lamp, and a window covered with faded grey curtains.

Kendy walked over to the window and pulled the curtains open, letting light flood the room.

"I'll take this room," I announced decisively. "And my current office can be converted into the reception area. Will that work?"

The suggestion seemed practical and a fitting change to mark a new chapter for the office.

"Sure will," Patricia agreed. "But I'll need some funds for Kendy and myself to go shopping."

"Kendy's got that sorted."

"I have an idea about the syringe," Kendy chimed in. "I know someone at a lab who might analyse its contents quicker than waiting for forensics."

"Who's that?" I asked.

"Niha Yang. We went to Uni together. She's with BioBot Industries, over in Jersey."

This new information seemed promising, potentially accelerating our understanding of what we were dealing with.

~ ~ ~

While Kendy and Patricia were out shopping for office furniture, I decided to contact Lucy Yip, assuming she was unaware of her blackmailer's identity. Carmen had given me Yip's number. The call went to her voicemail, so I left a message with my details.

Shortly after, Bulldog called with the toxicology report on Dwip.

The report was baffling: Dwip had died from a lethal dose of synthetic snake venom, something the lab had never encountered before and couldn't find on any international poisons database.

"Nanobots," I muttered, piecing things together. "It must be Yip's nanobots."

Bulldog sounded sceptical. "But how?"

"Kendy recalls Dwip mentioning that the nanobots could morph."

"Morph, as in shape-shift? This sounds less like a medical breakthrough and more like a bio-weapon."

"Exactly. It possible the murderer could inject the victim and then remotely alter the nanobots to mimic venom."

Bulldog was concerned. "So Yip might be testing a bio-weapon?"

"I don't think Yip is the perpetrator, but it's likely her invention. Someone with access to it is using it for nefarious purposes."

"We need to talk to Yip, get a list of everyone who could access this technology," Bulldog suggested.

"I just tried calling her, but got voicemail."

"Do you think she's in danger?"

"Possibly from Ren Tanaka, the blackmailer, and if the murderer is using her tech, she could also be a target."

"We need to narrow down our suspects. Let's speak with Yip as soon as possible," Bulldog proposed.

I agreed to stay on it. The analysis of the syringe now seemed less pressing, but as I was about to call Kendy to stop her going to BioBot Industries, my phone rang. It was Yip.

She was brief. "I'm in a meeting and can't talk. Can we meet later?"

"How about 8 PM at your lab?"

"That works. I'll send you the address."

As the day neared its end, I glanced at the clock; it was nearly 7 PM. Time had flown by in a whirl of activity and revelations. Just then, my phone buzzed with the text from Yip: 'Wing Ji Yip Lab, 6th Floor, 10 Washington Place, NYU Campus, in the Village.' It was conveniently just a fifteen-minute walk from the office.

Feeling the pangs of hunger, I decided to grab something to eat before the meeting. I quickly sent a text to Patricia, letting her know I'd meet her at my apartment around nine. With that, I grabbed my coat and headed out of the office, making my way towards the NYU campus.

CHAPTER
TEN

Kendy and Patricia had finished shopping, content that they had bought enough items for a substantial office makeover. Walking towards the office, Patricia had more ideas. "Before everything arrives, we need to have it painted and then re-carpeted."

"I've got just the right person for the paint job, the drummer in our band, Butch. And for carpet … I know, let's ask Linus, the owner of the Regis Building. He knows everyone."

They entered the Regis Building and knocked on Linus's door. After a moment, it opened.

"Well, am I the luckiest man alive or what? Two beautiful girls visiting me. Who's this flaming redhead, Kendy?"

"Linus, meet our new office manager, Patricia."

Taking Patricia's hand and wrapping it around his arm, he escorted her inside his apartment. "I can see I'm going to have to visit the office more often to try and win your heart."

"There will be a place for you, Linus," Patricia said, "I'll just have to make some adjustments and move Axis a little to the left to make room for you."

"Axis, do I detect the bounder is more to you than just your boss?"

"Patricia," Kendy said, "I'll go bring down your luggage from the office … we'll take a taxi to Axis's apartment."

Kendy took the elevator. Just as she got out, her phone rang. It was Niha Sang. Kendy explained about the syringe and needing its contents analysed. Niha offered to help by doing the analytics herself, claiming it would only take her an hour. She suggested Kendy bring the syringe to her lab at 9 PM, she could do it then because she'd be alone. Kendy agreed, and Niha texted her the address.

~ ~ ~

Ren was waiting for a call from Lucy Yip to confirm the blackmail arrangements, so when his phone rang, he jumped up off the bed, his heart pounding. He answered using a false tone to disguise his voice.

"Hello."

"Mr Tanaka, this is Florence Stein, HR for Wenden Securities. We've been unable to contact Jason Collins, and your number was listed for emergencies. He hasn't made his shifts and hasn't called. I wonder if you..."

His voice returned to normal. "Um, I'm in New York right now, let me check on him and I'll get back to you."

"Thank you, Mr Tanaka."

He sat back against the bedhead, worried that something had gone wrong. He quickly dialled the neighbour.

"Hello Dorris, this is Ren from next door. Have you seen Jason?"

"Oh, hi Ren dear. Don't you know? Oh my lord, the LAPD were all over the poor dear yesterday. They arrested him, handcuffs and all ... and he hasn't been back. It was just like a scene out of CSI..."

"Thanks, Dorris. I'm away at the moment ... it must have been a mistake. I'll ring the police and sort it out. Bye."

Now, he was in panic mode.

~ ~ ~

I exited the elevator on the 6th Floor and found the entrance to the Wing Ji Yip lab. The door was open, revealing an ultra-modern, unmanned reception area. As a door swung open, Yip stepped out looking swank, and gestured for me to enter her office. Inside, the luxurious office's walls were adorned with citations and diplomas. A wood-panelled feature wall showcased a stylishly lit display of trophies—Professor Yip was undeniably the real deal. With her black hair styled in a bob, her fringe broadened her face's appearance, yet it did not detract from her attractiveness. Dressed in a dapper blue business suit, she looked ready to cut a deal.

She settled into a small lounge setting, cross her shapely legs and motioned for me to take an armchair opposite.

"Mr Stone, nice to see you again," she purred.

"Axis would be good. Impressive setup, now I understand the five-hundred-dollar hourly rate for freelance work with the cops."

"Ha, yes, I wish I could charge that to the Uni. How can I assist you?"

She was quick to get to the point.

"I have numerous questions for you, Lucy. May I address you by your first name?"

"Certainly, go ahead, fire away."

"Some might be somewhat sensitive. My associate, Carmen Hu, mentioned you're touchy about certain topics."

"Perhaps, you'll soon discover."

"Okay, let's start with the Pussy app. Why did you create it?"

We locked eyes in a meaningful pause while she pondered her response.

"To raise capital."

"That seems a considerable effort for someone as successful as you, and risky?"

"No risk, nothing illegal. I'll be frank with you, Axis. I needed to raise two million dollars quickly to fund the final development of a technology I have a buyer for. This is outside my tenure with the University."

"The nanobots?"

"You're well-informed."

"Why appropriate the song from Lunatic Fringe?" I asked, glancing at her fringe.

She appeared shocked. "I appropriated nothing. I had an agreement with Dwip."

"And that was?"

"I could use the song, provided I re-recorded the vocals so it wouldn't be the band's. The rest of the band would have objected otherwise. Dwip understood my intentions and agreed I'd pay her every cent from the downloads after securing the sale. It was a win-win for Dwip and the band. She even supplied the backtrack."

"Do you have proof of this arrangement?"

"No, it was just between Dwip and myself."

"Did anyone else know?"

"Just my assistant."

"Who is?"

"Niha Yang. She works for BioBot Industries and assists me part-time. She's a former student of mine."

Alarm bells were ringing in my head. I leapt up. "Jesus!" I pulled out my phone and dialled Kendy. It went to voicemail. I then called Patricia.

"Trish, where's Kendy?" I was pacing the floor, Yip watching me with interest.

"She's delivering the syringe to her friend Niha at BioBot Industries in Jersey. Why?"

"I'll explain later, I'll call you back." I ended the call, sat down, and faced Yip. "We have a problem."

"What's wrong?"

"Someone used your nanobots to murder Dwip. It could only be you or someone from your office. It wouldn't be you, so it must be Yang."

"Oh my god, are you serious?"

"She attempted to kill Zola, then Rag Doll—apparently, she harbours a vendetta against the band. She lost a syringe, and Rag Doll found it. Kendy called Yang, being old friends she agreed to analyse it ... Kendy's with her now at BioBot."

"She might kill her. Look, Yang stands to earn ten million dollars from the deal. She introduced me to BioBot; they're purchasing it for one hundred million. All I had to do was produce a working model, which we've done. Yang will go to any length to protect her stake."

"She'll have to do more than eliminate Kendy. She'll need to get rid of Ren Tanaka too."

"Dwip's brother Ren? Why?"

"He's your blackmailer."

Lucy nearly toppled from her chair in astonishment. She clutched her forehead. "Oh my lord! Ren, but why?"

"He has multiple motives, including blaming you for his brother's death."

"He has no idea ... but how did he...?"

"His boyfriend is Jason Collins, the security guard who filmed you and Serina. He attempted to blackmail Serina, but we intercepted him."

"So he recognised me? He knew about the BioBot offer, thus deciding to blackmail me. If Yang learns it's him ... Wait, she's tracking his phone! Should I call Yang?"

I stood up swiftly. "No, I need to get to BioBot immediately!"

"I'll drive you, let's go."

~ ~ ~

Kendy met Yang in the Development Lab reception area on the seventeenth floor of BioBot Industries.

"Kendy, long time no see."

"Niha, yes, it's been a while since Uni and Professor Yip's classes."

"Let's head into the lab," Yang said, leading Kendy through large double doors. She switched on a light, illuminating a section of the vast room filled with technological equipment; the rest remained shrouded in darkness.

Yang paused under the light. "Everyone's gone for the day ... What have you brought?"

"A bizarre story. I work for a private investigator, and when my friend Sonoko was recently murdered..."

"I'm sorry to hear that," Yang sympathised.

"The killer struck again but left this syringe behind. We believe it contains the same lethal concoction that killed my friend."

"That's unbelievable. What an opportunity to prove that. What should we be looking for? I need to set the parameters on the analyser," Yang probed, seeking to gauge Kendy's knowledge.

"We suspect it contains nanobots capable of disguising themselves, currently masquerading as water."

"Remarkable. Never heard of such a substance. Who's the prime suspect, if you don't mind my asking?" Yang inquired nonchalantly, accepting the syringe from Kendy and placing a sample on a glass slide.

"Believe it or not, Professor Yip."

Yang looked back at Kendy, feigning astonishment. "You're joking!"

"And there's more…" Kendy showed Yang the video of Lucy and Serina on her phone. "The other woman is Serina Sun, the actress."

"I can't believe it. And the twist is, my deceased friend's brother saw the video and is now blackmailing the professor. You know him, Ren Tanaka, from our year at Uni."

"This is too much, Kendy. I need a drink. Let's put this in the liquid analyser; it'll take about thirty minutes. I've got a hidden bottle of wine in my office."

Yang inserted the slide into the machine, switched it on, and ushered Kendy into her modest office. She turned on the light, revealing a simple setting.

"Not as fancy here, take a seat," Yang said self-consciously, going behind her desk. As Kendy sat down, Yang opened a drawer containing a bottle of red wine, two glasses, and a bottle of Midazolam HCL syrup—a potent oral tranquiliser. She covertly added Midazolam to one glass, filled it with wine, handed it to Kendy, and then poured herself a glass. "To old times," she proposed, clinking glasses across the desk.

~ ~ ~

Lucy handled her Tesla adeptly, pushing it at breakneck speed in the Holland Tunnel before exiting into Jersey. She pulled up outside the twenty-storey BioBot Industries building, left the car in the no-parking zone at the front, and hurried inside, only to be confronted by a guard in the expansive, marble-encased lobby.

"Sorry, ma'am, you can't leave your car there."

"I'm Professor Yip, keep an eye on it for me," she commanded with authority and then led us past him towards the elevator.

We disembarked on the 17th floor and entered the lab. The lights were off; she flicked them all on. As I surveyed the vast room, Lucy checked Yang's office. Finding nothing.

I noticed a syringe on the benchtop and called out, "Lucy, Kendy's been here."

She hastened over. I held up the syringe, and she spotted a small green light on a machine.

"She's used the liquid analyser," Lucy observed, "they were here, alright."

My phone rang. I answered, recognising Kendy's voice. She managed only four words: "Freezing in Biobot lab."

"Hello? Hello?" That was all I got. I relayed Kendy's message to Yip.

"It's the subzero room! Quick!" Yip deduced.

We raced across the room to a large stainless-steel door. "She's in here."

Upon opening it, we found Kendy curled up on the floor, ice in her hair and eyebrows, her lips blue, shaking uncontrollably, and visibly groggy. We helped her out. Yip wrapped her coat around Kendy.

"To the car, quick. I'll turn on the heater," Yip said, pressing a remote.

By the time we got Kendy into the car, it was sufficiently warm to start thawing her out.

I looked into Kendy's big brown eyes. "I think we got to you just in time. Are you alright?"

She nodded, still shivering, and managed to rasp, "Hey, Lucy ... Yang spiked my drink."

"Ken," Lucy started compassionately, "Axis filled me in. I want you to know I had no part in Dwip's situation, babe. She gave me the song for the Pussy App, knew all about it. This is all Yang; she must be psychotic."

Kendy nodded again between shakes. "We used to call her Loony Tunes at Uni, remember?"

Lucy rolled her eyes. "I didn't know; I wish I had."

"Okay," I said. "So where is she now?"

"She wouldn't have expected me to wake up from the spike ... lucky I had my phone ... um, I told her about Ren. I'd say she's like gone after him."

"She'd definitely want to stop him. He could jeopardise everything by sending that video to BioBot. But how do we find him?"

"Wait," Kendy said, "I've still got the phone tracker Carmen gave me. We can track Yang's number."

CHAPTER ELEVEN

Kendy was tracking Yang's number. "She's on 11th Avenue." Yip was already steering towards Manhattan. Concerned Patricia might be worried, given I was an hour late, I updated her. I mentioned the empty fridge and suggested she visit the greasy spoon a couple of doors up for food. She had already checked the fridge and questioned its purpose, given its lack of food. I vowed to change my ways. Her response was definitive, "I'm not going to be responsible for you becoming responsible because of me." Her words, shared over speakerphone, lightened Kendy's spirits despite her discomfort.

Yip's phone rang just as I ended the call with Trish. Answering on the car speaker, Yip said, "Hello."

"So, have you got the money?" It was Ren.

I interjected. "Ren, this is Axis Stone. Listen, we're offering you a chance to drop the blackmail, or you'll end up like Jason. Understand?"

"She owes me," he insisted passionately.

"What do I owe you for, Ren?" Yip inquired.

"For what you did to my brother."

"I did nothing to your brother; he was responsible for his own actions," Yip countered.

"You drove him to it."

"Nonsense, Ren. You know your brother struggled with

depression. When things got tough, he resorted to the bottle or other substances..." Yip argued.

"Ren, it's Kendy. What Yip is saying is true. Dwip and I experienced similar challenges with Hero."

"Look, Ren," I appealed, "the most pressing issue is that the person who killed Dwip is after you ... right now!"

"Was that who tried to inject me earlier?"

"Yes, she's tracking your phone. So, transfer everything essential from your phone to your SIM, then discard the phone. Understand? But first, where can we meet you?"

"Johnny's bar. I'm heading there now."

"It's in the Village," Kendy noted.

Yip located it on the sat nav.

"Okay, get inside, dispose of the phone, and stay near people at the bar. Don't leave. We'll be there in fifteen minutes. Clear?"

"Okay."

~ ~ ~

Ren entered Johnny's Bar, transferring data from his phone as he walked. Once inside, he removed the SIM, snapped the phone in half, and handed it to the bartender.

"Dispose of this for me and I'll take a vodka on the rocks."

The bartender complied.

"That's a waste," a soft female voice commented.

Ren turned to see an Asian woman beside him.

"I'm done with technology," Ren said tiredly.

The girl extended her hand, "Cherry Matsuda, but everyone calls me Blossom."

"Hi, Blossom. I'm Ren Tanaka."

"Same heritage, huh? That calls for a drink. What are you having?"

"A vodka on the rocks."

"Make that two," Niha Yang masquerading as Blossom instructed the bartender.

~ ~ ~

By now, it was nearing 11 PM. With fewer cars on the road, the journey to Johnny's Bar in the Village promised to be quicker than usual. As we exited the tunnel onto Canal Street, Yip slowed down to turn left onto Greenwich Street, the most direct route to the Village. We were fortunate to catch the green light just as we reached the intersection. As we turned, a car traveling north on Greenwich Street ran the red light and collided with us. There was an almighty band—the airbags deployed instantly. The car rolled over twice, accompanied by the deafening sound of twisting metal and shattering glass. Eventually, we came to a stop. Silence enveloped me as the realisation of what had happened sunk in. These moments occur in seconds, yet they feel like an eternity, unfolding in slow motion. Voices outside the car sounded slurred, faces and hands appeared, blurred—I wondered if I was whole, and what about Yip and Kendy? The stark whiteness of the airbags, the confusion ... You've been in an accident? Was that my thought, or someone else's words? Then, a siren.

I awoke to the sound of rattling wheels, lights flickering past ... a person in green with a mask and a peculiar hat ... through a door ... hands, many hands, lifting me sideways ... then under an intensely bright light ... more faces, all masked.

~ ~ ~

Blossomed ordered a second drink. The conversation had been strange for Ren, awkward, but he was following Axis's advice: 'Stay with people until we get there.' Yet, he couldn't help but wonder where they were. Yang discreetly fished the bottle of Midazolam syrup from her pocket, deftly concealing it in her hand. She managed to remove the lid and, as Ren's attention momentarily drifted towards the door, looking for Axis, she spiked his drink. But luckily, Ren caught her reflection in the mirror at the back of the bartender. It suddenly clicked—the reason behind the awkward conversation.

Blossom was the murderer!

Realising waiting for Axis was no longer a viable option, Ren knew he had to escape immediately. He concocted a plan on the spot. Turning back to his drink, he reached for it, then deliberately knocked it over, spilling it on Cherry's lap. He leapt up, simultaneously apologising to Cherry and signalling the bartender. "Oh, hell, I'm so sorry."

Cherry stood up, clearly irritated but trying to remain composed.

The bartender handed her a towel, which she used to dab at her clothes.

"It's fine, it's fine," Cherry muttered and then excused herself to the ladies' room.

Seizing the moment, Ren placed twenty dollars on the bar and stealthily slipped out the door. Once outside, he sprinted away as fast as his legs could carry him.

~ ~ ~

At the rehearsal room, the band members were growing increasingly anxious about Kendy's absence.

"Call her again," Zola urged Rag Doll.

"I've already called her three times; it just goes to voicemail. Do you have her mother's number?"

Zola checked her phone and dialled. "Hello, Mrs Lee, sorry to call so late. It's Zola. We're at rehearsals, and Kendy hasn't shown up. I thought you might ... Oh, you haven't heard from her since this afternoon? Okay, no, no, don't worry." Zola shook her head in concern.

"What about Axis? Do you have his number? He might know," Rag Doll suggested.

"Good idea." Zola dialled and was surprised to hear a woman answer. "Hello, who is this? Oh, you're a nurse ... What? Oh my God! Yes, three of them: Lucy Yip and Kendy Lee ... I will. Thank you." Zola looked gravely at the other band members. "That was a nurse at Lenox Health ER in the Village. There's been a car accident involving

Kendy, Axis, and Lucy Yip. Kendy's okay."

"Let's get there," Butch said decisively.

"You better call Kendy's mum back, Bla," Slick advised while packing up her guitar.

Zola nodded in agreement.

~ ~ ~

The four Lunatic Fringe band members hurried along the corridor of Lenox Health to the triage area, where they found Patricia waiting nervously.

Rag Doll sat next to Patricia, taking her hand. "What's the news, Trish?"

"Axis and Kendy are still in ER; Yip is in casualty and okay."

"What happened?" Zola asked.

"They were in Lucy's car, turning from Canal onto Greenwich Street when another car ran a red light and T-boned them," Trish explained. "It must have been speeding; they rolled twice. The Tesla's airbags and it being an EV, with no fuel to catch fire, probably saved them. The other car wasn't an EV, and the driver was incinerated, the paramedics said."

"You must have gotten here quickly to see the paramedics," Butch remarked.

"They said Axis was trapped in the car, handed them his phone, and told them to call me. I got here as he was being loaded into the ambulance, so I rode with him," Trish explained.

"Was he conscious?" Rag Doll asked.

"No, that's what was really weird. Even when he handed them the phone and told them to ring me, he wasn't fully conscious. The medics think it was his subconscious directing them."

"Far out!" Rag Doll exclaimed.

A masked doctor emerged from ER and approached them. "Mrs McCloud?"

"Yes," Trish replied tentatively.

"Mr Stone is fine. Three broken ribs and narrowly avoided a

punctured lung. It's remarkable he survived such a devastating crash..."

"I know, I saw the Tesla. It was a mess," Trish said, visibly relieved.

"Ah, a Tesla. That explains it ... no gas, no fire," the doctor said, his eyes smiling behind his mask.

"What about Kendy Lee, doctor?" Zola inquired.

"She was in the back seat and well-protected. She's fine, just needed a thorough check to ensure everything is internally intact. So, just bruises and scratches ... And Miss Yip, not being particularly tall, was spared any serious injury. Just bruised thighs from the collapse of the steering wheel, and a concussion ... They'll all be discharged tomorrow."

"Thank you, doctor," Trish said, her relief palpable.

~ ~ ~

Walking as if I had just swallowed a live lobster whole, Trish assisted me towards the office door. The past two days had felt like an entire month—one day in the hospital and another flat on my back in the apartment. We paused at the door, which featured the beautifully inscribed script on frosted glass: 'Stone, Vargas and Chan Investigations, LLC.' I was taken aback; the office already sported a new look. Trish opened the door, revealing a totally modern, upmarket reception area.

"Wow," was all I could manage, genuinely impressed. She guided me into Kendy's office, where she sat at her new desk. Kendy looked up and joked, "Hi boss, you're walking like you forgot to remove the butt plug!"

"I'm not complaining," I retorted with a chuckle. Looking around, I noticed the plush crimson carpet, beige walls, a lounge area, and an abstract painting that looked like the workings of Kendy's mind—the place looked fantastic.

"Butch did the paint job," Kendy said, standing to join us.

They escorted me to my office door, then Kendy opened it.

Stepping inside, I was greeted by sunlight streaming through the window. One wall was lined with bookshelves filled with my dad's books and other reference materials. The carpet was a royal blue, and there was a three-seater brown leather Chesterfield lounge with two matching armchairs. An antique mahogany desk sat in the room, accompanied by a large, comfortable brown leather office chair. Behind the desk hung the Stone family portrait, previously in my old office, now reframed. My investigative certifications from both Australia and the U.S. flanked it. It was smart, stylish, or as we Aussies would say, 'schmick.' I sat in the new office chair. "It fits just fine. Girls, we're on the map. You did a terrific job."

"It was mostly your new PA, Mr Stone," Kendy admitted.

"She's got class, taught her everything I know," I jested.

"Yes, he did indeed, that took all of five minutes," Trish quipped back.

"Plus, I've got some news," Kendy said flopping onto the lounge, Trish beside her. "Ren survived and was last seen by the bartender at Johnny's Bar, bolting out the door after spilling his drink on a customer I believe was our Miss Yang. I expect Ren's back in LA now. Lucy got the okay this morning on her deal with BioBot, and Bulldog called ten minutes ago. He's arrested Niha Yang and is charging her with first-degree murder ... and, we're playing tonight, and you're totally expected to be there."

"I will, but no dancing," I ordered with a chuckle.

CHAPTER
TWELVE

The fractured ribs made dressing a challenge, and I had to enlist Trish's help. As always, she was accommodating, and we both ended up looking quite presentable, though Trish outshone me with her stunning appearance.

The gig was at 'The Bitter End' in the Village, a venue almost like a second home to the band. Kendy had recommended we arrive early, anticipating a large crowd. She had left our names at the door and reserved a table for us. I was particularly eager to see Kendy perform; it would be my first time experiencing her talent as a musician.

It's funny how appearances can be deceiving—my mum didn't look like a novelist, either. It just goes to show, you should never judge a book by its cover.

While Trish was adding the finishing touches to her makeup, I received a call from Bulldog.

"How are the ribs?" he asked.

"They only hurt when I laugh or try to roll over in my sleep."

"Getting dressed must be fun. I broke a couple in a fight once and have bloody hay fever. Can you imagine sneezing with broken ribs?"

"Not much fun. What's up?" I asked.

"Just wondering what time the band's playing tonight?"

"Ten, why?"

"Thought I might drop by. You going?"

"Sure am. It'll be good to catch up socially."

"Why not. Leave my name at the door so I don't have to flash my badge to get in."

"Just one?"

"Yeah, I'm big enough for two but, no, just me," he joked. "You heading out now?"

"Yep. Kendy said it'll be packed. See you there."

"Who was that?" Trish asked, joining me.

"Bulldog. He's coming tonight."

"That's great. I'm keen to meet him."

"You look too good to take out," I commented, admiring her from head to toe.

"Don't call me fast food, young man," she joked.

I took her arm, and we left to catch an Uber.

Pulling up outside the venue, it was evident that it was going to be a big night, with a line stretching around the block. Devon Steel, standing at the entrance, waved us through. I always felt a bit guilty about the VIP treatment, but I wasn't going to complain.

Inside, we were ushered to a prime-positioned table, where I received the surprise of my life. Seated there were Charlie, Carmen, Enzo, Danny, Miranda, Lucy Yip, Booker, Linus, Kendy's mum, and Bulldog. Bulldog's earlier call now made sense; he had been gauging my arrival time to orchestrate this surprise. I glanced at Trish, who rolled her eyes, a silent admission of her role in the scheme.

"Well, look at all you lovely rogues!" I exclaimed.

"And here comes one more," Trish added.

Nick came over and gave me a bear hug that was painful but welcome. "Kimosabe," he greeted.

"Tonto!" I replied. Just as I mentioned the only person missing, Carlos appeared with a tray of beers. I was so moved I had tears in my eyes. My friends' efforts to be here meant the world to me.

We settled into our seats as the lights dimmed and a single spotlight illuminated the centre stage. Devon stepped into the spotlight, approaching the microphone.

"Welcome, punters. It's a special night in honour of one of our own who we lost. Sonoko Tanaka, affectionately known as Dwip, was the keyboard player and composer of 'Femme Fatale' and other songs in the band's repertoire. She will be deeply missed—we all loved Dwip. Taking her place is a longstanding friend of the band, Kendy Lee, who brings her own compositions, some of which you'll hear tonight. So without further ado, give it up for The Lunatic Fringe!"

The band burst onto the stage, launching immediately into a power-packed punk song. I was astounded by Rag Doll's dexterity; she leapt about the stage reminiscent of Anthony Kiedis in his heyday with The Red Hot Chili Peppers.

After a few energetic songs, the spotlight shifted to Kendy as she prepared to sing her new composition, "Rita."

There by a bar room window
stands a silhouette
Of a hard-cold lover
Above her
Her name
A raunchy claim to fame,
The portrait of the
Queen of Sunset Strip

Rita, when the smoke clears
When the smoke clears
You shine
But your cut and cold talents
Where your crime

Rita, when the smoke clears
When the smoke clears
You shine
But your blunt and bold tactics
Where your crime

> Stripping of your clothes rose
> A chill to the spine
> A thrill to all who saw you...
> Show your wears, show your wears
>
> Showing it all was
> against the law
> But they misread your art
> sweetheart
> And they branded you a whore
>
> Rita, when the smoke clears
> When the smoke clears
> You'll shine
> But your blunt and bold tactics
> Where your crime
>
> Rita, when the smoke clears
> When the smoke clears
> You'll shine
> But your blunt and bold tactics
> Where your crime
>
> So, back then ... Hollywood blushed...

Kendy initiated a Charleston-style instrumental vamp on the keyboards, effortlessly transporting the audience back to the roaring 1920s in their imagination. Seamlessly, she then transitioned back into the chorus.

> Rita, when the smoke clears
> When the smoke clears
> After all these years
> You're still showing it all,
> Up there on the wall

Rita, when the smoke clears
When the smoke clears
After all these years
You're still showing it all,
Up there on the wall

Rita, Rita, Rita

We were completely captivated by her sultry voice and the enchanting song. As it concluded, Kendy received a standing ovation, and I could see her blushing even from our distance. The tempo shifted once more, and the stage lighting transitioned to evoke a sunny Californian atmosphere. Rag Doll, taking the lead, announced, "That was 'Rita' by Kendy. Up next, another new one, 'Contribution.'"

You know, life wasn't meant to be easy
but that don't mean, we can't work it out.
When the good times get expensive.
We all walk the walk in fear of doubt.

Why don't we just laugh about it,
instead of paying a shrink to work it out?

Hmmm, I've got a contribution
it certainly ain't new.
Forget about all that worry
Just get on with what you do.

Why don't we just laugh about it
instead of paying a shrink to work it out.

Maybe I just lust for life
but you know I think that's kind of nice
seeing it through...
Ooo hoo ooo...

Nothing really seems that bad
and even when you're feeling sad
the sky turns blue ... ooo hoo oo...
you know a smile will always see you through.

I hope you dig my reasons
It's so easy to feel down.
There's too much convenience
for your feet to hit the ground.

Don't take life for granted
we spend a long time dead
Stand up and be counted
proud of everything you've said.

Maybe I just lust for life
but you know I think that's kind of nice
seeing it through
Ooo hoo ooo ...

Nothing really seems that bad
and even when you're feeling sad
the sky turns blue ... ooo hoo oo...
you know a smile will always see you through.
yeah, you know a smile will always see you through.

The new song 'Contribution' got people up and dancing. In the midst of the lively atmosphere, Rag Doll called out, "Up on stage, Pussy App!"

Lucy rose to the occasion, making her way through the enthusiastic dancers and up onto the stage. She was handed a microphone just as the band seamlessly segued into 'Femme Fatale.' Together, Lucy and Rag Doll sang the song, their voices harmonizing perfectly.

G. L. Keady

Once a fool always a fool I'm told
After the show, aficionado.
Hangout man, your backstage plans are cold
Openings unfold, aficionado.

I've had it up to here
You thought that you had me
You didn't see the tear fall
Fall as you left me
Well, I don't want to know, know, know, aficionado
I don't want to know, know, know, aficionado

I've had it up to here
With all the games
You dressing-room lovers
Drive me insane

I don't want to know, know, know, aficionado
I don't want to know, know, know, aficionado

You made me your fool
That's your golden rule
You told me to quit
So I held on a little bit
Arrr-har!
I see you lying there
With your iron eyes
I feel you choking me
Femme fatale surprise
Arrr-har!

I don't want to know, know, know, aficionado
I don't want to know, know, know, aficionado

The performance of 'Femme Fatale' was a resounding success,
eliciting thunderous applause from the audience. We all loved it.

While I half-expected an encore, the stage took an unexpected turn as Devon joined Rag Doll under the spotlight. The applause eventually subsided, and Devon made a special announcement. "Tonight, we've got a very special guest in the house. No, he's not a rock star, nor is he a famous actor … In fact, he's not only a private detective but also one terrific bloke. We'd like to dedicate this next song, sung by Kendy, to Mr Axis Stone."

I felt a mix of embarrassment and curiosity about which song they would play. As soon as the opening notes filled the room, I recognised it immediately. Despite my broken ribs, I stood up, reached out for Trish to join me, and, against my better judgment, we danced. The music was just too compelling to resist.

Oh wow, wow, wow!
When I first saw you, sitting there
My heart it skipped a beat.
And when I burst across the dance floor
I had wings on my feet

What to say
I wasn't sure
Hey, have I seen you before?
Say, say no more -
Say no more mon amour, mon amour
Say no more...

Let me kiss your lips
We'll take our kicks
Talking the mumbo jumbo
Talking the mumbo jumbo
Dancing the terrible tango. Hey!

So we danced
Into the night
Held tight and cheek to cheek

And when we saw
The dawn was breaking
We were tired, we were weak

What to say
I wasn't sure
Hey hold on tight mon amour
Say no more, say no more
Mon amour, mon amour
Encore!

Let me kiss your lips
We'll take our kicks
Talking the mumbo jumbo
Talking the mumbo jumbo
Dancing the terrible tango. Hey!

Kendy gestured for me to join her on stage. As I made my way up, I was greeted with my white Fender Stratocaster, all plugged in, tuned, and ready to go. Embracing the moment, I played the solo, letting each note resonate with the energy of the room. Then I joined in on the vocals.

Quiero lamer tu cuerpo
Susurrar en su vido...
Quiero lamer tu cuerpo
susurrar en su vido

Quiero lamer tu cuerpo
Susurrar en su vido...
Quiero lamer tu cuerpo
susurrar en su vido
Dancing the terrible tango

Let me kiss your lips
We'll take our kicks

Talking the mumbo jumbo
Talking the mumbo jumbo
Dancing the terrible tango.

Let me kiss your lips
We'll take our kicks
Talking the mumbo jumbo
Talking the mumbo jumbo
Dancing the terrible tango.

Let me kiss your lips
We'll take our kicks
Talking the mumbo jumbo
Talking the mumbo jumbo
Dancing the terrible tango. Hey!

Quiero lamer tu cuerpo
Susurrar en su vido…
Quiero lamer tu cuerpo
Dancing the terrible tango!

The audience was thoroughly energized. After my performance, I stepped down from the stage and returned to my friends at the table. Trish, with a look of curiosity, asked, "That was your ringtone, wasn't it?"

"Sure was," I confirmed.

"Who wrote that song?"

"The Terrible Tango?"

"Yes."

"I did, years ago, with my old mate Tony."

Patricia looked at me, clearly impressed. "A man of so many talents," she remarked.

After the band finished their final set, Yip invited our table backstage for a special gathering she had arranged. The spread was far from ordinary—it was a catered affair with champagne, caviar, and an array of culinary delights.

Amidst our praises for the band, the distinct sound of a spoon tapping a glass garnered everyone's attention. Lucy, glass in hand, stood up.

"Hey everyone, can I have your attention for a moment?" she requested.

The room quieted down, all eyes on Lucy.

"Most of you know about the infamous Pussy App I created with Dwip's help to sell downloads of 'Femme Fatale.' Many think it was written about me, but it wasn't. The true muse will remain Dwip's secret. She allowed me to use the song, even providing a backtrack. I recorded a vocal and used AI to alter my voice, creating the Pussy character. The goal was for downloads of the song to fund the development of my nanobot technology for BioBot Industries. Today, I've signed a contract with them for one hundred million dollars." Whispers of astonishment rippled through the crowd. Lucy continued, "This technology aims to cure diseases and is intended only for peaceful purposes, not as a bio-weapon. I agreed to repay Dwip from the earnings if the deal succeeded. So—" She pulled an envelope from her pocket. "In honour of this commitment, and with gratitude, this envelope contains two bank drafts. One for a million dollars made out to The Lunatic Fringe, and..." she paused, gesturing towards the door, through which to everyone's astonishment stepped Ren Tanaka. "One for a million dollars made out to Sonoko Tanaka, going to her only remaining family member, Ren Tanaka."

Ren was visibly moved, his tears undeniable. Only a day before, he had attempted to blackmail Lucy for a million dollars, and now she was selflessly gifting it to him. Applause filled the room, leaving few eyes dry.

Professor Lucy Yip had truly come through. Yang faced justice, and Charlie announced that Serina Sun was dropping charges against Jason, who would soon be released from jail. The only person left sombre was Kendy, consoled in a corner by her mother, Linus, and Book. Joining them, I said to Kendy, "I lost a friend and a musical mentor, Powelly. His incredible talent and the essence of who he was live on in me. I hope you find the same solace, Kendy."

Together, we raised our glasses in a toast to Lucy. Rag Doll, with a heartfelt smile, led the salute: "Cheers to the girl with the lunatic fringe."

Coming Soon:
"CAT STREET"

Book Eight in the Axis Stone Mystery Series.
Stay tuned for another gripping adventure!

The song lyrics were reproduced in The Lunatic Fringe
with the permission of Keadybros. Music Publishing.
http://www.keadybros.com

RITA
(Gary L Keady and John D Phelps)

CONTRIBUTION
(Gary L Keady and Rodney J Keady)

THE TERRIBLE TANGO
(Gary L Keady and Tony J Rees)